Dedication

For my wife, Elaine,
with all my love

Acknowledgments

This book has been a "work in progress," although I only came to that conclusion after sifting through years of scripts, columns, photographs and memorabilia. I am indebted to many of my colleagues and friends who have supported me as both a broadcaster and a journalist.

My special thanks to Gail Pike, Wendy O'Keefe and the staff of Creative Bound and Jayne and Cliff Anderson and the staff of *Today's Seniors* for supporting me as a writer. My sincere gratitude to Rich Little and Bill Luxton for their many thoughtful considerations. My thanks to my radio co-workers, who contributed in various ways to the production of my programs, Pat Carty, Dale Schwartz, Ray Eckford, George Roach, Bill Paton, and Dick Maloney—and to the staff and management of radio stations CFRA/CFMO-FM, Ottawa.

I am grateful in so many ways to my children, Suzanne, Mary Elinor, Michael, Paul, Peter, Gregory, John and their families, for their years of love and support. Most of all I want to thank my wife, Elaine, who is my proofreader, grammarian, personal editor, typist and computer operator. Without her inspiration, loving input and patience, this project would never have been completed.

CONTENTS

FOREWORD

Gord Atkinson has always been to me Mr. Show Business. He has seen more stars in his life than Carl Sagan. I have known Gord for nearly 40 years, and he is one of my dearest friends.

When I was growing up in Ottawa, Canada, Gord had a radio show called *The Campus Corner*. It was a teenage music show, with Gord playing all the hit records and talking to a lot of kids. I used to appear on the program occasionally and do impressions.

On his award-winning program *Showbill* he featured exclusive interviews with legendary entertainers. It was a top-rated show for an amazing 36 years, and in my opinion one of the best hours ever produced for radio. I was always pleased to be one of his guests.

To me Gord possesses all the qualities that make a good interviewer; he knows his subject, he listens to what they have to say and he asks interesting questions. I used to tape a lot of his interviews on a little 50-dollar tape recorder and used these tapes to develop my impressions of many of the celebrities he spoke with. Once Gord even interviewed a young Elvis Presley. Over the years, the radio station either lost or erased the tape. I found my copy of it years later, Gord restored it and today it is a prized collector's item.

We share a lot of the same interests: a love of show business, an interest in people and a fascination with entertainers. I've had the pleasure of introducing many celebrities to Gord, but not Bing Crosby. Gord introduced me to Bing, and what a lovely man he was. Gord not only became a close friend of Bing's, but became a leading authority on his life. In fact, I always say, "Gord, if your life ever flashed before your eyes, you wouldn't be in it—Bing would."

Gord Atkinson has talked to hundreds of stars. My contribution to these interviews was not only getting him introductions, but making sure he knew where he was going for the interview and what time it was supposed to start and asking if he had batteries for his tape recorder. (Of course, I'm a great one to talk—I need a road map to find my way home.)

I'm very happy Gord is writing this book. Many of the people he talked to are gone, but they are not forgotten. Through this glimpse into their personalities, I hope younger people will get a chance to know why we loved and held them in such esteem. Thanks, Gord.

Your friend,

Rich Little
Las Vegas, Nevada

The Road to Hollywood

I am sometimes asked how it was possible for a local broadcast-journalist to meet and interview over 200 famous show business personalities.

Through the efforts of considerate friends, notably Rich Little, Bing Crosby, Paul Anka and songwriter Sammy Cahn, many doors were opened for me and meetings arranged with prominent performers and legendary stars. Their managers and agents put me in contact with many more well-known entertainers.

In a career that has spanned five decades I have traveled extensively and recorded many of my interviews in Hollywood, Las Vegas, Palm Springs, New York and London, England. With the advent of the portable tape recorder I was able to interview celebrities in any place, at any time, at their convenience.

With the exception of my radio documentaries that have been syndicated internationally, my programs and columns have been produced and written primarily for the two Canadian markets that have been my home base, Toronto and Ottawa.

The celebrity status of my interview subjects and the caliber of our radio anthologies brought these programs to the attention of Columbia University in New York, the U.S. Association of National Catholic Broadcasters, the New York International Radio Festival and the Canadian Association of Broadcasters, for special recognition and awards.

Whenever I have had the privilege of meeting a well-known and respected performer I like to think that I am conducting an interview on behalf of my listeners or readers, and asking the questions that would help them to gain a better insight into the person being profiled.

It was my relatives and their friends' interest in the arts and entertainment which brought me to an early conclusion that, as Irving Berlin stated, "There's no business like show business."

I was born April 20, 1927, in Toronto, and although I was a child of the Depression years I had a very happy and comfortable childhood. My parents gave me love and a sense of security. My father, Art, was a fire fighter and a World War I veteran who had been wounded twice in action. His rare reminiscences of that "war to end all wars" always captured my imagination. I was especially intrigued by his memories of "the soldiers in greasepaint," like the Dumbells, who entertained behind the lines, and I was captivated by the songs that were popular during those dark days.

Our vacations were spent at the rural residence of my Dad's sister Annie and her barber husband, Jim. They lived with their three children in a big old house in the village of Newcastle on Lake Ontario. Their home could have been a model for the Waltons' house on the popular TV series. The hard economic times of the 1930s denied them and many country folk the amenities of life, including indoor plumbing and electricity. Yet I look back now with only happy memories of those idyllic summer months, living the life of Tom Sawyer by day and joining the family at night for storytelling and sing-alongs by a bonfire on the beach.

In 1933 my mother, Eleanor, through the consistent efforts of my Dad, won a trip to the Chicago World's Fair. Her account of "A Century of Progress" (the exposition's theme) and the lure of the "windy city" impacted on her six-year-old son as if she were relating *Tales of the Alhambra.*

Her cousin Hazel lived in New York City, and whenever she visited our home I was enthralled by her accounts of life in what Walter Winchell called "Baghdad on the Hudson." As I grew older I was fascinated by her stories of working in major hotels in Manhattan and Atlantic City and meeting celebrities of the day. She was especially pleased that when the Dorsey Brothers Orchestra was featured at her hotel she became quite friendly with Tommy and Jimmy and their devoted mother. Then there was a night she never forgot, when the infamous Al Capone arrived at her hotel (to the consternation of the staff and management) with his entourage for a late night dinner. Gangster films were very popular at that time, and the nervous employees were fearful that as a result of being in the presence of the burly mobster they might suffer the same fate as the characters in those underworld movies.

Since my grandparents had passed on by the time I was ten years old, my mother's Aunt Mary, who was an incurable film-goer and the matriarch of our family, was my surrogate grandmother. To her many nieces and nephews she was our beloved "Aunt Mamie." Attending the movies with her was always an experience; she refused to wear glasses for her failing eyesight, and out of necessity we had to sit in the front row of the theater. To this day when I enter a cinema, I feel a pain in my back and my neck from crouching in my seat and straining to look up at the screen. But it was worth the discomfort inflicted on my young body to be treated to an early evening at the "picture show."

Aunt Mamie was a knowledgeable movie fan and followed the private lives of the stars. While watching a film she would keep up a running commentary on the off-camera goings-on of the actors and actresses we were watching on the silver screen. Her "Irish whispers" were distracting, but she paid our admission fee and I would never complain about her movie chatter.

My father was only an occasional patron of the neighborhood theaters, but my mother was always available for a film or two each week. Between my aunt and my mother, I was hooked on the flicks at an early age. But I was never happy attending Saturday afternoon matinees—the kids were too noisy and rambunctious for a serious young film aficionado who was trying to memorize dialogue and follow the action on the screen.

My only personal connection to show business was on my mother's side of the family. Her oldest brother, Harold, and his wife, Dolly, produced and appeared in variety stage shows during the vaudeville era. He also took on the role of Santa Claus for Toronto's annual department store Christmas Parade.

There were other talented and, I suspect, frustrated performers in the family. They didn't have to be coaxed at our social functions to entertain. Uncle Willy, who was an accomplished amateur tap dancer,

often said that "they jockeyed for position" to sing their songs, tell their jokes and perform before their captive audience of relatives and friends.

A quick study, Uncle Willy perfected his tap routines by memorizing the steps of the dancers who performed in vaudeville. He taught me my basic "shuffle off to Buffalo" and "old soft shoe." His greatest thrill was seeing Bill "Bojangles" Robinson in person.

The English entertainer Des O'Connor once said to me: "You know, there is raw talent in almost every family, but it takes someone to give these really talented people a push to break into show business." His comment was certainly true concerning several of my talented relatives who may have lacked the drive to pursue a career on stage, and received little if any encouragement from their friends and associates.

Looking back, I realize now more than ever that my mother's family of individualists and colorful characters could have been the inspiration for a Neil Simon play. I still miss those dear hearts, and am thankful to them for introducing me to the fascinating world of show business, and for giving me a collective family push to pursue a career that has brought me great pleasure and satisfaction.

New York, New York—A Magical Town

In 1939 the Great Depression had come to a merciful end, and despite war clouds in Europe, people in North America looked to the future with optimism and hope.

Appropriately, the dynamic, colorful and fabled city of New York welcomed the global community, as it staged the greatest show on earth. Never before had there been an international spectacle on such a grand scale as the New York World's Fair of 1939-40 with its imposing centerpiece the Trylon and Perisphere. Confidently and bravely it was acclaimed as the "World of Tomorrow."

It was during this turbulent period that I had my first encounter with the lure of show business in the metropolis that came to be known as "The Big Apple." I was in my last year of grade school, when my parents and one of my great-aunts planned a motor trip to glamorous Gotham, and told me I would be going with them! For a 12-year-old showbiz buff it was a dream come true. I quickly became the envy of my classmates.

While my family was of modest means and without a vehicle, my mother's widowed aunt, Kathleen, had a big 1929 touring Cadillac—but no driver. My father's motoring credentials as a member of the Toronto Fire Department were quite impressive, and he frequently operated the car for her pleasure and ours.

Our accommodation on Long Island was guaranteed at an apartment in Queens shared by my mother's cousin Hazel and her roommate, Margaret (I "properly" referred to both ladies as "my aunts").

As we embarked on what was at that time considered a long journey, our Toronto neighborhood seemed light years away from magical Manhattan. By the time we approached the great metropolis, late at night, I was finding it difficult to keep awake. But my mother made sure I was alert as we crossed the newly opened George Washington Bridge, knowing that I didn't want to miss our first view of the fabled skyline.

While my youthful enthusiasm for the sights and sounds of that bygone holiday have been clouded by the passage of time, some impressions and observations are still clear in my mind.

Many cities today compete with New York's modern accomplishments, but in 1939 it was truly the city of the future. Of its many wonders the graffiti-free subway trains of the BMT and IRT topped my list. We traveled quickly and securely all over New York. The underground was not a haven for crime but a system where locals and tourists alike moved safely. It was our main mode of transportation, and on the occasions when the ladies went shopping, my father and I used the trains frequently.

One of our stops was the harbor where we viewed the magnificent sight of two great liners, *The Normandie* and *The Queen Mary*, side by side. *The Normandie*, painted in its peacetime colors, never left port and perished in a dockside fire near the end of the war. *The Queen Mary*, now a floating hotel at Long Beach, California, had been painted battleship gray, and would soon begin its many trans-Atlantic wartime crossings. We watched the sleek *Ile de France*, with tugboats as an escort, leave port.

From Battery Park we all viewed the Statue of Liberty for the first time; strolled safely through Central Park, where we visited the greatly acclaimed zoo; walked late at night along 42nd Street to Times Square (where only pickpockets were a major cause for concern in those more innocent times); and took in the pleasures of Coney Island's amusement park.

My New York "aunts" worked at the Lexington and Park Central hotels. At the former we attended our first Polynesian Revue with Lani McIntyre's company direct from Hawaii. The music of "the islands" was all the rage of Manhattan. Across from the Park Central Hotel we toured Carnegie Hall, and had lunch nearby at a popular forerunner of Colonel Sanders, The Bird in Hand. But I was even more fascinated with a neighboring eating establishment called The Automat. At this revolutionary cafeteria, for just a few coins dropped into slots, out would pop sandwiches, drinks and dessert.

In more recent years my trips back to that part of Manhattan have left me with a warm glow of nostalgia, especially when visiting a songwriter friend of mine, Irving Caesar. His apartment suite was located in what was the old Park Central Hotel.

A few blocks from that venerable hotel, we experienced another highlight of our 1939 holiday by attending a movie and stage performance at the world-famous Radio City Music Hall. The film featured Leslie Howard and a sensational young Swedish actress (in her first English-speaking role), Ingrid Bergman—it was the classic tear-jerker *Intermezzo*. The picture put the ladies in a state of rapture. My father was fidgety throughout the screening—and I fell asleep! However, the precision work on stage of the high-stepping Rockettes brought us (and the audience) to our feet, applauding loudly.

Coincidentally, my first date was arranged for my Manhattan sojourn by my chaperoning "aunts." Her name was Dorothy, and she was an "older woman" of 14. We attended the rodeo at old Madison Square Gardens, and most memorably, the New York premiere engagement of *The Wizard of Oz* at Loew's opulent mid-town theater, where we were captivated by another Dorothy as she took us down "The Yellow Brick Road."

The World's Fair at Flushing Meadow was a fairyland of gardens, fountains, modern architecture, restaurants, foreign pavilions, beautiful walks, theatrical events and a wondrous amusement park. Transportation throughout the fair, by various methods, included motorized trams whose horns tooted the first few notes of "The Sidewalks of New York" as they passed pedestrians along the way.

Billy Rose's Aquacade, which introduced Esther Williams, and Frank Buck's Jungleland were the major spectacles, but my favorite entertainment was at a re-creation of Little Old New York with its horse-drawn carriages, gaslights and a turn-of-the-century saloon.

Not until Montreal's Expo '67 was there an international extravaganza that equalled New York's exposition of 1939-40. Even the New York sequel of 1964-65 (at the same location) suffered by comparison.

Following a day at that marvelous fair, we would take the subway back to our apartment and (since minors accompanied by adults were admitted to taverns) stop off at a neighborhood bar, The 11 O'Clock Club. There the adults would request a favorite song from the resident tenor, and the two friendly bartenders would serve us our nightcaps. They always served my soda pop with a flourish and addressed me in a warm and amusing manner as "The Coca Cola Kid."

It was all so long ago, that October in 1939, and yet it remains far more than just a memory.

"A nightcap" at The 11 O'Clock Club, New York City, October 1939. (left to right) Aunt Kathleen, my mother, "the Coca Cola Kid" and my Dad.

Route 66 to Hollywood

August 14, 1945, was a day to remember. On that date unprecedented celebrations took place around the globe to mark the end of the horror and devastation of World War II. The unrestrained joy of that day is still vivid in the minds of those who are old enough to "remember when." Members of the armed forces and civilians alike can recall, years later, where they were and who they were with, and how they spent the last day of the war.

For me it was the most memorable time of my young life. I was an 18-year-old soldier and had just completed my training in the Canadian Infantry. As an incurable movie fan, I had hoped to someday visit southern California, and when I was given an extended leave in late July of that year, I seized the opportunity to hit the "Road to Hollywood." Traveling from my home-town Toronto to Los Angeles in uniform afforded me every courtesy and consideration, from special rail and bus rates to affordable accommodations.

If my first visit to the movie capital had been the inspiration for a morale-boosting wartime movie, it would have been quickly rejected by the critics as celluloid fiction. The people I met and the things that happened seemed far removed from reality.

It began with a train trip from Toronto to Chicago. Along the way a group of young ladies boarded the coaches to distribute sandwiches to service men and women and promote their Michigan city, which was made famous by Glenn Miller. The wax paper wrappings covering the sandwiches proudly contained the words of the big band hit, "I've Got a Gal in Kalamazoo."

After staying overnight at a Chicago U.S.O. hostel I decided to continue my westward trek via Greyhound bus, so that I could get a closer look at the cities and countryside along the way. Appropriately, the two records that I heard playing on juke boxes at almost every stop we made were the Bing Crosby hit versions of "Route 66" (which I traveled for "more than 2000 miles from Chicago to L.A.") and "On the Atchison, Topeka and the Sante Fe," from the Judy Garland film *The Harvey Girls.* The movie was inspired by the pioneer innkeeper Fred Harvey, whose adventurous staff opened the first chain of hotels across the southwest.

The stark and fascinating desert of New Mexico and Arizona with its Silver Sands, Petrified Forest, Painted Desert and Grand Canyon was a beautiful and awesome sight to behold. There were few divided highways back then, and the single-lane Route 66 was a lifeline for the residents of towns and villages along the way. It was not an uncommon sight to see Navajos in their distinctive native dress flag down a bus, pay their fare to the driver, ride for several miles and then get off in what seemed like the middle of nowhere.

Some images remain with you throughout your life. Crossing the mountains of California with its valleys of welcoming citrus groves remains a graphic and colorful picture in my mind. The sweet odor of their orange blossoms was intoxicating.

Just as exhilarating were my days and nights in Hollywood, where being in uniform gained me entrance to the movie and radio studios. When I arrived at the Los Angeles bus terminal I was delighted to read in a local paper that my favorite star, Bing Crosby, was in town for the summer, appearing before the Paramount cameras in an Irving Berlin musical called *Blue Skies*. An enthusiastic teenage fan, I was determined to somehow see Bing in person. I soon had that opportunity, when I volunteered to be one of a group of servicemen who would be responsible for crowd control at a celebrity fund-raising golf tournament for the Hollywood Guild Canteen. I was mesmerized following the Crosby foursome, and watching the effortless play of Bing, I soon forgot my responsibilities and for most of the match became part of the crowd. I managed to get Bing's autograph, and took a few candid photographs of him in action.

Later that week I attended an armed forces radio show called *G.I. Journal*, with Bing as the mythical paper's editor and Claudette Colbert as his secretary. The amusing plot had Bing looking for an office boy, and a lean young man named Frank Sinatra applying for the job.

Bing Crosby Enterprises was located on Sunset Boulevard near Beverly Hills. On a typical sunny California day I hitched a ride out to the Crosby Building. It was a three-story structure where Bing's varied business interests were managed. The building is still standing, with the Crosby name over the entrance. It sat alone back then, but is now surrounded by retail stores and offices.

As I arrived I saw an elderly man standing by the front door. I approached him and asked him politely if he knew if pictures of Bing might be available at the reception desk. He assured me that they were and invited me to come inside the building, where staff members addressed him as "Mr. Crosby." We took the elevator to the third floor and he escorted me to Bing's office, where he handed me an autographed photo from Bing's desk.

I was flabbergasted at that moment and blurted out, "Are you Bing's father?" He proudly told me that he was and I immediately asked him for his autograph. He smiled and said, "Why would you want my autograph, I'm nobody." To which I replied with fan fervor, "Yes you are—you're Bing's Dad!" A very pleasant man, he signed my autograph book: "To Gordon, Sincerely your friend Harry L. Crosby Sr."

Years later Bing told me that he always left autographed photos on his desk for fans who might drop by. He also told me that he called his father "Hollywood Harry." It seems his Dad was always promoting his movies and records and would show any passer-by the latest clippings about his famous son.

My persistent efforts to gain entrance to Paramount Pictures paid off when I first entered the gates of the studio with a group of servicemen. We were escorted to the sets of films in production, including an Alan Ladd adventure drama set in *Calcutta*, and met the very popular star of the 1940s. While touring from one sound stage to the next film set, Bing came out of a studio door and walked toward our group. He was wearing a chef's hat for a scene in *Blue Skies*, humming a melody and snapping his fingers. He immediately put us at ease with a few jokes about his pal, Bob Hope. He asked me where I was from, and when I replied "Toronto," he said with a grin, "You had Hope up that way recently, didn't you? Pretty dull time, huh?"

A week later, August 14th, I was feeling rather depressed when I realized I had lost my autograph book, containing personal greetings from several of the top stars of Hollywood's halcyon days. While I was standing outside the servicemen's hostel where I was staying, a long white convertible pulled up, and the driver asked me if I wanted a lift. He was a kindly, older man, who seemed to sense my dismay. When I told him of the loss of the autograph book, he tried to put my mind at ease by telling me that he was one of the makeup men at Paramount.

We drove through the fabled gates of Paramount, waving to the guard on duty, and parked near the studio commissary. I could hardly believe my good fortune—I felt like a latter-day "Merton of the Movies." My considerate host took me to lunch, where I recognized cafeteria customers who were reigning stars of the era, including Robert Cummings and Barbara Stanwych. Supporting players and extras, wearing a variety of costumes and in makeup, were seated throughout the room or were in the self-serve line-up.

Following lunch my new-found friend escorted me to the Crosby dressing room. Bing was standing outside the door talking to a rising young singer-actress, Olga San Juan, who had a feature role in *Blue Skies*. When they had finished their conversation, Bing walked toward us, and surprised me by telling me that he remembered meeting me from the week before. At that point the makeup man began to tell him about the loss of my autograph book. Then there was an amusing exchange as Bing said to me, "You were wearing a different uniform," and in my confusion I referred back to the autograph book and said, "I lost it." With tongue-in-cheek he replied, "What, the uniform?" and I stammered, "No the autograph book"—and we both laughed. (I was wearing my regular uniform, having sent my summer uniform to the cleaners', following a mishap with chocolate ice cream.)

The makeup man had to leave us for a few minutes and Bing invited me into his dressing room. Trying to make intelligent conversation, I asked him about his recording plans and future films. As he lit his pipe, I thought about the many times I had seen that ritual in Crosby movies. Overwhelmed at being in the presence of the world's most popular performer and my boyhood idol, I blurted out, "Gosh! the folks back home will never believe this!" In his mellow baritone he replied, "Sure they will." Sensing my awe he then asked me if I was free for the rest of the day, and if so, would I like to watch some of the scenes being shot for *Blue Skies*. Upon my reply that I was free and would be honored to be his guest, he suggested that he would have a photo of the two of us taken later that day. He then excused himself to study some of his lines, and I was taken by the makeup man (who had returned) to the main studio, where I watched the late Billy de Wolfe and another rising actress, Joan Caufield, film scenes for the picture. I also had a chance to say "hello" to the incomparable Fred Astaire.

By mid-afternoon radio news reports could be heard all over the lot, and it was obvious that the war in the Pacific was about to end. While it had been evident for some time that universal peace was only days away, when the end came at approximately 4:00 p.m. Pacific Coast Time, August 14, pent-up emotions burst like a tidal wave over Los Angeles.

It seemed that everyone at Paramount headed for the studio square, site of a war bond billboard with large images of Hitler, Mussolini and Tojo. A big letter "X" had been painted over the first two caricatures. Suddenly voices began calling for Bing, which eventually broke into a chorus of "Crosby, Crosby, Crosby." A few moments later Bing

"The folks back home will never believe this!" Bing Crosby and an 18-year-old fan outside his dressing room at Paramount Studios, the day the war ended, August 14, 1945.

appeared carrying a bucket of black paint and a brush. A ladder was put in place and Bing began climbing toward the billboard. While all this was happening I had been carrying on a conversation with a friendly fellow standing beside me, without taking my eyes off Bing. Only when my companion made a comment about the height of the sign and Bing's dexterity, did I realize that I had been having a spirited conversation with Alan Ladd!

With two sweeps of his brush Bing placed an "X" over the effigy of Tojo, and the crowd let out with a loud cheer—and took off in every direction to celebrate. Despite my own joy that the war was over, I was very concerned that in the excitement Bing would forget the photo. I waited for him outside his dressing room. I soon became dejected, however, when the studio appeared to be abandoned. Just as I was about to leave, convinced that I had missed the opportunity for a rare photo with Bing, he arrived around the corner with a photographer. "I had a difficult time finding one of these fellas, so we'll have to take it right away," Bing said.

Across the street from his dressing room there was a backdrop for the wartime action film *Calcutta*. Bing looked across at the rubble from a battle scene, gave me a nudge in the ribs, and just as the cameraman clicked his shutter, he quipped, "I see they're finally getting a new dressing room for Hope."

Shortly after my return home the picture arrived with a personal autograph, which read: "To Gordon, with every good wish, Bing Crosby." It was the beginning of our friendship—a friendship that lasted 32 years, and afforded me the privilege of producing and hosting the radio anthology of his life and times, *The Crosby Years.*

When I left Paramount on that fateful day I was "walking on air." A few hours later I went to the Hollywood Canteen, and despite top entertainment and an impressive turnout of stars that night, after the events of the day, it was almost anti-climactic. Standing on the steps of the famous U.S.O. landmark, I struck up a conversation with the prominent character actor Elisha Cook Jr., watched the Phil Harris Band march up the street and enter the Canteen, and later stood in the packed building while Marlene Dietrich and Bette Davis danced with the more outgoing Allied servicemen.

August 14, 1945, was indeed a historical day to remember and savor, especially for the men and women of our armed forces who served with great distinction and bravery overseas.

By strange Hollywood coincidence it was also the day that I decided I should pursue a career in the entertainment business—a decision that has brought me pleasure, fulfillment, happy memories and most of all, many wonderful friends.

Meeting Hollywood's Founding Father

In the development of the motion picture industry no one was more closely associated with its capital than the legendary film maker from Ashfield, Massachusetts, Cecil B. DeMille. His name was synonymous with Hollywood. In a historical sense, DeMille was the founding father of the movie capital. He was already a film pioneer when he left New York in 1914 for the west coast. Attracted to southern California's open spaces and agreeable climate, he rented a barn in the middle of a citrus field on the outskirts of Los Angeles. It was there that Hollywood was born when he filmed a revolutionary six-reeler called *The Squaw Man.*

DeMille's films were movie milestones, dating from the silent screen years to the era of wide-screen projection and stereophonic sound. His name on a cinema marquee was a bigger drawing card than the names of the famous stars who appeared in his pictures.

He was fascinated by the biblical figures that his clergyman father extolled from the pulpit of their fundamentalist church, and brought them to the screen in spectacular epics. His biggest box-office hits were inspired by the prophets and evangelists: *King of Kings*, *The Sign of the Cross*, *Samson and Delilah* and of course, *The Ten Commandments*, which he filmed twice, once as a silent in 1923 and again as a film classic in 1956. His other memorable movies included a 1934 version of *Cleopatra* with Claudette Colbert, and his 1952 Oscar winner *The Greatest Show on Earth.*

In the summer of 1945, during my unforgettable visit to California, I was hopeful that I might be successful in gaining entrance to the

Hollywood studios. With a Canadian sailor that I had befriended, I spent a frustrating morning trying to gain admittance to Paramount Pictures. The guards at the famous Marathon Street Gate kept telling us that we had to know someone inside in order to visit the sets. As we were about to give up our post outside the studio walls, a long black limousine pulled up to the curb and a very familiar figure got out. He was carrying several parcels as he crossed the street.

In teenage disbelief I said to my sailor buddy, "That's Cecil B. DeMille!" To which he replied with an incredulous look on his face, "You're nuts! Why would DeMille be carrying his own parcels?"

With a bravado and temerity known only to the young, I greeted the renowned movie maker and told him of our unsuccessful assault on the gates of Paramount. To our sheer delight he told us to follow him and he would see what he could do. Much later I had cause to feel chagrin when I realized that in my excitement I hadn't offered to carry his parcels.

DeMille had his offices adjacent to the Paramount lot with a separate entrance from the street. When his mammoth productions were before the cameras he would have the walls between Paramount and RKO removed to accommodate his casts of thousands.

As we entered his waiting room he invited us to have a seat while he met with his staff. A few minutes later a group of American servicemen, who had seen us enter the building with our famous host, arrived in the lobby in hopes that they might also gain admittance. We were fearful that, being part of a larger group, we might lose our advantage. However, Mr. DeMille emerged from his office, looked at us and said, "I see your ranks have grown. But, that's all right, my secretary has agreed to take you around the lot." (It was during this visit to Paramount that I first met Bing.)

Our pleasure at finally gaining entrance to a major studio was only exceeded by our joy at meeting Mr. DeMille—Hollywood's most famous citizen. For years we had heard his highly distinctive and mellifluous voice on the soundtracks of his films, and as the host of radio's most popular drama series, *Lux Radio Theatre*, and now here he was introducing us to his personal secretary.

Upon our return to his office from a star-studded tour, he answered our questions and talked about his films. He even explained to us how he went about choosing the titles for his pictures. On the wall adjacent to his desk hung a cork board with pieces of paper pinned to it. On each piece of paper was written a possible title for a new movie. The project he was working on at that time was the story of the drawing of the Mason-Dixon line. He was leaning toward the title *Unconquered*, which he admitted he had misspelled. Paulette Goddard had already been signed, but Gary Cooper was undecided about his participation.

In a rare moment of candor, he told us that he thought Cooper would appear in his film, then added: "But Gary is like a little boy, he puts his foot in the water to test it, and quickly pulls it out. So, you're never sure until shooting begins if you've got him."

C.B., as he was known in the industry, had a reputation as a hard taskmaster who was the bane of actors and a tough disciplinarian with those behind the cameras. The middle initial "B" was for an unusual family name, Blount, but around Hollywood his associates thought it might have more properly stood for "Boss" or "Ballyhoo." Some of the veteran actors that I've interviewed confirmed his reputation as a very demanding and difficult employer.

But, on that August day so long ago, he was a most congenial father figure and a warm host to a group of appreciative young men in uniform. Why, following our long tour, he even invited us to "use his facilities." Considering our surroundings we felt as if we had received an invitation to a tiled Shangri-La!

Mr. DeMille was 78 at the time of his death in 1959.

Starstruck in Hollywood

The summer of 1945 was a magical time in the land of make-believe. It was Hollywood's halcyon era and the golden age of radio and the great motion picture studios.

At CBS and NBC I attended several broadcasts, including the *Screen Guild Players* starring Lionel Barrymore, *The Adventures of Ozzie & Harriet, The Great Gildersleeve, Blondie* and *Art Linkletter's House Party*.

At the Hollywood Bowl I attended a concert under the stars. The great Maestro Leopold Stokowski was on the podium for the first half of the program. A pops presentation followed, with Johnny Green conducting for soloists Frank Sinatra, Frances Langford, Danny Kaye and Claudette Colbert. Miss Colbert was the narrator during the playing of a suite from Walt Disney's *Bambi*. It was the first time I had witnessed thousands of people holding matches and lighters aloft while they flickered in the dark night air. It was quite a sight, a display of audience participation instigated by Danny Kaye.

Through perseverance and luck I gained entrance to the famous film factories of MGM, Warner Brothers, United Artists, RKO, Disney and Paramount.

At Warners Cary Grant was appearing as Cole Porter in *Night and Day* and Errol Flynn was starring in *Never Say Goodbye*. Two of the screen's most colorful villains were also before the cameras, Sydney Greenstreet and Peter Lorre. Lorre, when he realized a group of servicemen were on the lot, ran from his dressing room to give us his autograph. In contrast to his screen persona, he was a very considerate and friendly man.

I have two vivid recollections of my day at MGM. While visiting the set of a whimsical drama, *The Hoodlum Saint*, co-starring William Powell and Esther Williams, a studio photographer snapped a picture of me and my Canadian sailor friend getting Powell's autograph. The popular star of *The Thin Man* series looked at us with a smile and said, "Well boys, there's a photo for posterity." He was as gracious and debonair in person as he was in his many films, which included *Life with Father*, *My Man Godfrey* and *Mr. Roberts*.

My other sharply etched memory at Metro happened on the set of what became a classic motion picture, *The Postman Always Rings Twice*. While watching Lana Turner and John Garfield shoot a scene, I noticed the bobby-sox idol of the era, Van Johnson, tip-toeing into the studio. As soon as the cameras stopped rolling, I approached Johnson, knowing that I couldn't return home if I didn't get his autograph for my teenage cousin, Lois. As he wrote her a personal autograph I said in appreciation, "Gee, thanks Mr. Johnson—this will be worth a million dollars to her." To which he replied with a twinkle in his eyes, "I wish it was to me!"

Fifty years ago the urban decline of Hollywood had not begun and it was indeed the "land of make-believe," especially for an impressionable young movie fan.

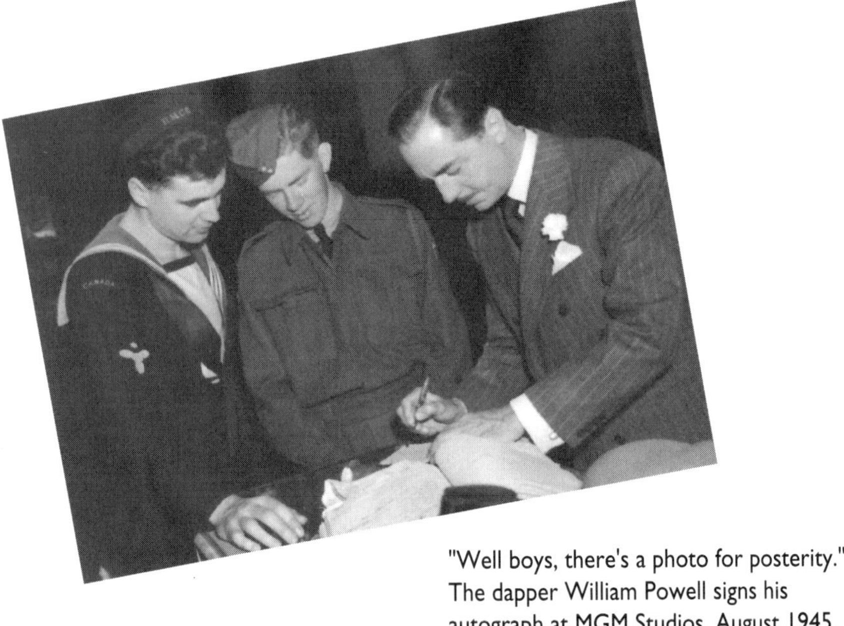

"Well boys, there's a photo for posterity." The dapper William Powell signs his autograph at MGM Studios, August 1945.

On the Showbiz Beat

In the theater actors often talk about "coming down" after an exhilarating performance. They find it difficult to adapt to reality and need a period of time to adjust to their surroundings. When I returned home to Toronto from my star-studded trip to California, I knew exactly how they felt.

After being discharged from the army, I spent little time planning my future and more time regaling relatives and friends with tales of my adventures in Hollywood. I was determined to someday return to the "Golden State." But fate often changes youthful dreams. Like millions of servicemen across North America, I took advantage of continuing my education at the government's expense. Even though I was only a short time in uniform I had enough credits to take a year-long course in journalism. The hastily formed post-war rehabilitation center that I attended was the forerunner of the Ryerson Polytechnic University. Never a serious student, I nevertheless found the prospect of a career in the media an appealing proposition.

My education up to that point had taken me from elementary school to De La Salle Oaklands, Toronto, a boy's military college where I was taught by the Christian Brothers. My musical background began and ended there, playing a snare drum in the school's highly regarded bugle band and appearing in the chorus of a student production of *H.M.S. Pinafore.*

Once I had completed my journalistic studies I was unable to find employment in my chosen field, and for a couple of years worked as a clerk for the National Cash Register Company. To this day I wonder how I kept that job, since I spent more time writing and submitting radio scripts than I did promoting and punching cash registers.

Occasionally someone asks me how I got into radio. It was my father who coaxed and cajoled me to answer a newspaper ad from a private radio school. It was staffed by veteran broadcasters and opened around the same time that Lorne Greene founded his radio academy. Among the well-known performers who were broadcast students in Toronto at that time were Leslie Neilson, Gordie Tapp, Fred Davis and my old pals, Les Lye and Bill Luxton.

While attending my broadcast studies at night, I finally broke into show business when I joined the staff of the Ontario distributors of Compo Records. I was hired as a writer-publicist and "go-for." Compo held the rights to the Decca label throughout Canada.

During that same period I had taken on the position of president of the Canadian branch of the Bing Crosby fan club. In this role I found myself at odds with a policy of my new employers. It was a ruling that by today's business methods seems ludicrous. Compo officials felt justified in preventing radio stations from playing Decca records on the air. They were convinced that if people could hear their records on the radio they would not go out and buy them.

Frustrated at not being able to hear Bing's Decca records on local radio, I wrote to him and his brother-manager, Everett, explaining the broadcast ban. They were supportive in their replies and assured me that they would have no objections to his records being broadcast.

With their encouragement I contacted the Compo policy makers and requested permission to begin a 30-minute Toronto program of selections from Bing's vast Decca library. To my surprise and delight they agreed, but only for a once-a-week show, reserving the right (for the time being) not to lift the ban for general air play.

Supported by my fellow Crosby fans I approached the most listened-to radio station in Canada, CFRB. Despite my obvious broadcast deficiencies they accepted my proposed program and services. I was offered $15.00 a show to produce and host the *Club Crosby*, which was endorsed by the fan club of the same name. Despite the small remuneration, my relatives were impressed that I would receive that much money "for 30 minutes of work." The program was heard Saturdays at 5:00 p.m. and ran for two years on CFRB, and then moved to CHUM Radio where it continued for four more years. It was also broadcast by the magic of magnetic tape on CFRA, Ottawa.

During my time at CFRB, I did my first celebrity interviews. In 1948 the renowned orchestra leader Paul Whiteman, who was known as "the King of Jazz," conducted a Gershwin concert in Toronto. As all Crosby fans know, it was Whiteman who discovered Bing and had him, Al Rinker and Harry Barris form his Rhythm Boys.

It was a few years before tape was in common use and my conversation with the great man was broadcast live from our studio. Remembering my inadequacies at that time, I am relieved that the interview was not recorded. (Eventually I did have one of the programs recorded on a transcription so I could hear what the show sounded like.)

Anyone who appeared on the *Club Crosby* program received a fan club pin, and I have treasured photos of my pinning them on actor Robert Cummings (who was a golfing buddy of Bing's) and the one and only Robert Hope. It was the first time I met Hope, who was a 1949 headliner at Maple Leaf Gardens. He looked down his famous nose at the Crosby pin and gave an appropriate sneer.

On January 2, 1950, I was hired full time by radio station CHUM, where Lorne Greene broadcast his student radio dramas. I was hired as an announcer-librarian and eventually given the assignment of showbiz reporter. I met and interviewed visiting celebrities, including Jimmy

"Boy, was I nervous!" Pinning a Bing Crosby fan club pin on Paul "Pops" Whiteman. My first celebrity radio interview, October 1948.

Actor Robert Cummings receiving a fan club pin and guesting on the *Club Crosby*, April 1949.

Bob Hope "looks down his famous nose" as I point to a Bing Crosby pin on his lapel. Maple Leaf Gardens, Toronto, September 1949.

Durante, Hoagy Carmichael, George Murphy, Tony Martin, Jane Powell, Gene Nelson and a young Merv Griffin who was singing with the Freddy Martin Orchestra. Two of my co-workers, actor-comedian Larry Mann and sportscaster Phil Stone, who were my radio mentors, have remained close friends.

While I was making modest strides in the entertainment business, my personal life was unfolding like the script of a "boy meets girl" film. Elaine De Rose wasn't the "girl next door," but she was the girl across the street. Being more than four years older than she I was hardly aware of her growing up. So I was surprised when I received an invitation to attend her 16th birthday party. Although her mother and my father had agreed that I should attend, to my family's dismay I rejected the idea of spending an evening with a "bunch of young kids." My Great-Aunt Mary's reaction to my decision was swift and dramatic, telling me that if I didn't attend "it would disgrace our family." I thought at the time that she had seen too many movies. My mother insisted that I at least cross Lansdowne Avenue and tell her mother that I wouldn't be attending. Fortunately her Mom wasn't at home.

My knock on their door was answered by the prettiest girl I had ever seen. For me it was love at first sight! Four years later on September 3, 1951, we were married. We were both only children who were blessed

"The girl across the street, Elaine DeRose." Our wedding day, September 3, 1951, St. Helen's Church, Toronto.

Our first attempt at a family portrait, September 1965. The photographer had to wait for Elaine to stop a nose bleed—and I ran out of gas on the way home.

Our children clockwise, from Elaine's lap, Mary Elinor, Paul, Peter, Gregory, John, Suzanne and Michael (*Citizen*—UPI photo).

with a big family—two daughters and five sons, and at last count, eight grandchildren.

Elaine's Dad, Charlie, who was a master tailor and professional musician, played flute and piccolo on stage and with studio bands in the early days of radio. Born in Italy, he influenced me greatly with his love of opera and classical music. He also made me my first tuxedo for those on-stage appearances that were coming my way. He and his wife Mary gave me their love and support to such an extent that I felt as if I had a second set of parents.

After six years on the Toronto entertainment scene I accepted a position in 1954 as entertainment editor at CFRA Radio, Ottawa. In 1967 I became station and program manager of sister station CFMO-FM. My 36 years with the company brought me into contact with visiting celebrities, and eventually led to my on-location interviews and

Pictured from left to right: (son) Paul, his wife Suzanne; son-in-law Bob, his wife (daughter) Suzanne; dad and mom; (bride-daughter) Mary Elinor, husband David; (son) John, his wife Calère; daughter-in-law Rachelle, (kneeling in front, son) Michael; daughter-in-law Debbie, (son) Gregory; and kneeling to the left of Michael, (son) Peter.

syndicated radio programs, most notably, *The Crosby Years*, which has been broadcast around the world.

Over the years I have been a columnist for both the *Ottawa Citizen* and *Ottawa Journal* and a frequent TV contributor. Since 1989 I have been a featured entertainment columnist with Canada's leading newspaper for readers 50-plus, *Today's Seniors*.

The profiles that follow represent a cross-section of my exclusive interviews with actors, comedians, directors, musicians, dancers, singers and songwriters that I have been privileged to meet and interview—all celebrated personalities from the "Golden Age of Entertainment."

A group of journalists visit Fred Astaire during the filming of *Finian's Rainbow*. I'm the one without a tie. Warner Brothers back lot, August 1967.

THE LEGENDARY FRED ASTAIRE

Fred Astaire transcended the status of a legendary star—he was a 20th century phenomenon! Top hat, white tie and tails will for years to come be not only his trademarks, but the icons of a unique and phenomenal career. He was the embodiment of elegance and sophistication, giving new meaning to the words grace, style and class.

In private life, however, he was a simple, shy man, who was uncomfortable in crowds, and reluctant to talk about his personal life and amazing accomplishments.

One of my most memorable radio interviews took place at his hillside estate in Beverly Hills. Entering his home, I was understandably concerned about my ability to carry on a proper and meaningful conversation with him. To my surprise and consternation, he appeared to be uncomfortable when I turned on my tape recorder. It was a period when he shunned the limelight, and hadn't granted an interview in several years. However, he seemed at ease when we began to reminisce.

At the time of our meeting I was producing my radio anthology on the life and times of his friend Bing Crosby, and it took gentle persuasion from Bing's brother and public relations manager, Larry, before he agreed to the interview. I was told by Mr. Crosby that "Mr. Astaire will meet with you if you agree to discuss only his personal and professional relationship with Bing. He doesn't want to talk about himself."

It was the summer of 1974 and I was in Las Vegas for interview sessions following assignments in Los Angeles. A phone call from Larry Crosby took me back to L.A. After an overnight stay with our friends Larry and Gloria Mann, at their San Fernando Valley home, Larry drove me to my Astaire appointment. The address was so secluded, we only found our way with explicit instructions and a detailed map.

The Astaire estate was situated on a picturesque hill overlooking Benedict Canyon. His beautiful California-style mansion featured an attractive and practical circular foyer. Two of the rooms off the foyer were a sunken living room and a cozy den. Our interview took place in the den, which was laden with an impressive collection of books and record albums, and had a handsome pool table as a centerpiece with an adjacent bar. Floor to ceiling windows looked out on a kidney-shaped pool. The view from the den was spectacular—a broad vista of the canyon below.

At the time of our meeting, Fred Astaire was leading a quiet and, I believe, lonely existence. It was the period before he met his second wife Robyn Smith. He had been a widower since 1954, and for several years had led a very private life. Eventually he returned to the screen as one of the star-hosts of MGM's *That's Entertainment,* Parts One and Two, and for TV assignments as an actor, emcee and "talk show" guest.

Although he was reluctant to dwell on the past, his fond memories of Bing brought forth warm and amusing anecdotes. During the wartime years, while touring the European front lines, they often found themselves in both humorous and dangerous situations. "Once, while a troop convoy was taking a break," he told me, "Bing absent-mindedly went to light up his pipe and was set upon by panicky soldiers who extinguished the pipe and told him he was in the midst of trucks loaded with explosives!"

On one of my visits to the Crosby San Francisco estate, Bing recalled one of his favorite recollections of that same U.S.O. tour. They were billeted for several days in a remote French town, and went unnoticed by the local residents—until one morning at breakfast, a waitress excitedly ran into the mess holding a prewar movie magazine in her hand with a photo of Astaire and Ginger Rogers on the cover. Bing said, with a chuckle, "Fred was an instant celebrity, and I was practically ignored. He really topped me in that little French town."

On occasion when Astaire was asked by reporters to name his favorite dancing partner, not wishing to offend his leading ladies, he sometimes would reply "Bing Crosby." It was an answer he gave only half in jest. "We got along very well," he said with affection. "He's a great man, Bing. A very special person and it was a thrill to work with him. We had a lot of laughs together; he is very funny. He used to go out of his way to oblige me and make certain that I was happy with our work. He was in a class all by himself." They last worked together in 1976 in London when they recorded a wonderful collection of old and new songs for my producer-friend Ken Barnes. It is available on a compact disc on the EMI label with the appropriate title, *How Lucky Can You Get.*

In Hollywood's Golden Age they co-starred at Paramount in two musicals, *Holiday Inn* (1942) and *Blue Skies* (1945). In both pictures they did a song-and-dance routine. Astaire was amused that the casual Bing, who usually shot his musical sequences in one or two takes, rehearsed his steps over and over, and limbered up with exercises and weights for their dance routines, "I'll Capture Your Heart" and "A Couple of Song and Dance Men." On the other hand, Astaire, who was a perfectionist, rehearsed every musical scene until it was flawless. Bing told me that for one routine in *Holiday Inn*, the famous firecracker dance, "Astaire did 22 takes. To me the last one looked similar to the first, but not to Fred, who saw something that he felt wasn't right in each successive take."

The firecracker dance was done with small explosives called torpedoes that discharge when thrown against something hard. It was a spectacular scene in the movie and an Astaire classic. "That was a favorite of mine too," he told me. "It took a great deal of preparation. I had real torpedo firecrackers in my pockets and I threw a lot of them during the rehearsals. The cameras had to be close to the ground and when I began throwing them on the floor and they burst, the men working the lights and cameras were being sprayed by the sand in the explosive. They called out to stop the action and wipe their faces clean. They were then given big goggles for protection for their eyes. But it was a kind of kick to hear the torpedoes explode on the beat of the music. It was really a complicated and very tricky dance to stage."

My first Astaire encounter was at Paramount Studios during the production of *Blue Skies*. As I walked through the lot "star-gazing" I passed him walking alongside his bicycle; he stopped and said "hello." His movements were so graceful that the bike seemed to be floating alongside him.

Fred Astaire was born into a musical family, November 26, 1899, in Omaha, Nebraska. His father, who had emigrated from Austria, played the piano. His American-born mother enrolled him and his sister, Adele, into the best dance academy in New York. By the time they were teenagers they had become a professional team and were billed as the Astaires, since they felt their real name, Austerlitz, sounded too much like a battle. Their big break occurred in 1917 when they won a spot in an Ed Wynn show called *Over the Top*. Soon thereafter they became the "talk of Broadway," starring in *Lady Be Good*, *Funny Face* and *The Bandwagon*.

While appearing in London's West End, Adele met and married an English nobleman and retired from the stage. Returning to New York, Fred launched his solo career in 1932 in *The Gay Divorcee* in which he introduced Cole Porter's "Night and Day." Hollywood soon beckoned and he was given a small role in a 1933 Joan Crawford film, *Dancing Lady*. That same year he was teamed for the first time with Ginger Rogers in *Flying Down to Rio*, which featured the first song to win the Oscar, "The Continental." They became the screen's most popular dance team, appearing in a series of nine box-office hits throughout the 1930s. They were reunited in 1949 at MGM in *The Barkleys of Broadway*.

He was not only the most popular dancer of all time, but a master of light comedy and a very competent dramatic actor. He once said: "I kind of approach everything with enthusiasm because I only accept things I really want to do." His private life was beyond reproach. He was a devoted husband and father to his first wife, Phyllis, who died of cancer, and to his children, Fred Jr., Ava and Peter.

In 1980 he married Robyn Smith, an accomplished equestrian whom he met through his love of horses and racing. She was by his side at their home when he succumbed to pneumonia, June 22, 1987. Upon hearing of his death, Mikhail Baryshnikov said, "He will be a never-ending legend."

In 1967 I was one of a group of entertainment journalists visiting Warner Brothers Studios, where the filming of Astaire's first musical in many years was taking place—the screen adaptation of a very successful 1947 Broadway show, *Finian's Rainbow*. It was the one big disappointment of his unparalleled Hollywood career. He and his co-star Petula Clark (who was appearing in her first major movie musical) had high hopes for the picture. However, the critics thought the show, 20 years after its New York debut, looked "dated" on the screen and that it had lost some of its original charm. Francis Ford Coppola, who a few years later won the Academy Award for his *Godfather* films, was the director. For me, it was an opportunity to have a brief conversation with the always elegant Fred Astaire.

During the taping of our 1974 interview at his home, he was interrupted by a phone call from the son and daughter of two old friends, Jack Haley Jr. and Liza Minnelli, who were married at that time. He was very pleased to receive their call from New York and talked fondly about Liza's mother Judy Garland, who was his co-star in the Irving Berlin musical *Easter Parade*.

At the conclusion of the interview I asked him if someone could order me a taxi. To my surprise he replied, "I don't think you can get a cab up here. But I could drive you down to the Beverly Hills Hotel and you could get one there." The thought of driving through Beverly Hills with the inimitable star as my chauffeur set my mind in mad motion, wondering if I could somehow alert the media, and have this fantasy event filmed for posterity—or at least for home town coverage. My spirits were quickly subdued when he thought for a moment and added, "I'll check with the girls." Obviously his staff had occasions to order taxis.

Returning from the kitchen to the den (which he did with the same graceful steps that he always displayed on the screen) he told me that a cab had been ordered, but it would take some time for it to arrive and invited me to join him for a drink in his lovely sunken living-room. We had a very pleasant conversation about current affairs, his trips to Canada and his admiration of the then Canadian Prime Minister, Pierre Trudeau.

Fred Astaire was as charming and gracious in person as he had been in his well-remembered films. Shortly before leaving his hilltop home I requested a memento of my visit—a personal photograph. I took a picture of him standing by his library bookcases, which is a visible reminder of a day I will never forget.

When my taxi arrived at the Astaire estate, the cabby was stunned to be met at the door by the legendary star, who asked him to wait a moment while we finished our discussion. The speechless driver did a double- and then a triple-take, as he looked on in amazement while we concluded our conversation and my famous host bid me farewell.

As I entered the cab the "star-struck" driver finally found his voice, but could only say one thing: "Fred Astaire! What a guy! Has he got class!"—a statement that he kept repeating over and over. When he dropped me off on Hollywood Boulevard, to browse through the cinema book stores before my flight back to Las Vegas, I left him with his own words. With just a touch of humor and a great deal of sincerity, I said to him: "Fred Astaire! What a guy! Has he got class!"

My personal photo of Fred Astaire. A memento of my visit to his home in Beverly Hills, July 1974.

A commemorative photo with James Stewart, following our interview at his home on Roxbury Drive, Beverly Hills, March 6, 1984. We were socializing in the garden. (Photo by Rich Little)

"A Wonderful Life"

The warmth, conviction and sincerity of James Stewart, and his ability to portray a wide variety of screen roles, has won him unbounded critical and public acclaim throughout his career. He once said that he thought movies ideally should be "little pieces of time that people would never forget." The late Grace Kelly, who was his leading lady in Alfred Hitchcock's *Rear Window*, summed up his screen appeal best when she said that "his characters live with us and in us."

Hollywood made him famous and wealthy, but like the character he portrayed in one of his favorite films, *It's a Wonderful Life*, his small-town upbringing taught him that no man is a failure who has friends—and in that respect, Jimmy Stewart is "the richest man in town"!

Because of my friend Rich Little's close friendship with the Stewarts,

James Stewart

I was privileged to meet the greatly admired actor for the first time in 1976 on a Las Vegas TV special. In 1984, I had the pleasure of interviewing him at his lovely Tudor-style home in Beverly Hills. I reminded him that Rich has often said that the voices he does best are the voices of the people he admires the most—and there is no one Rich admires more than his boyhood movie idol.

James Stewart Home.

"The feeling is mutual," he replied, "I have great admiration for Rich; he is a master of his craft. He does my voice and mannerisms so well that people now tell me that I remind them of Rich Little! You know, when he first came out here, I was so amazed at his impression of me that I thought about adopting him, but my wife wouldn't go along with the idea, she said she couldn't live in the same house with two fellas kind of mumbling and talking real slow."

The Stewart movie characterizations have included real-life and fictional cowboys, detectives, newspaper reporters, military figures, businessmen, politicians, a famous musician, a circus clown, and even an imaginary rabbit's best friend in the light-hearted comedy *Harvey*. His roles have always touched the hearts and emotions of movie fans around the world.

The prestigious honors presented to the self-deprecating and down-to-earth star include the Academy Award, five Oscar nominations, the Kennedy Center Medal and the American Film Institute Award.

When he returned to Hollywood after World War II, his director-mentor Frank Capra was waiting with an idea for a film that he felt was made-to-order for his homecoming—the story of a small-town man, down on his luck, who thinks he is a failure until his unlikely-looking guardian angel convinces him that his life has been worthwhile.

Their heartwarming collaboration, *It's a Wonderful Life*, received mixed reviews when it was released in 1946, and was only a modest box-office success. With the advent of television, however, it became a TV yuletide favorite, viewed by families year after year. Today it is universally acclaimed as a Christmas classic.

He takes great pleasure in its success: "It's amazing and gratifying that it is shown all over the world at Christmas time. It does reflect the spirit of the season, and it has a happy ending that takes place on Christmas Eve. And it is true that it was inspired by just a few lines on a Christmas card that the Capras received. Frank was deeply moved by its message, that 'no man is a failure who has friends'—and that was all he had for a plot when he gave the idea to two wonderful writers, Frances Goodrich and Albert Hackett, who collaborated with Frank on the script."

Two earlier Capra films established the young James Stewart as a reigning Hollywood star. The 1938 movie adaptation of the zany Broadway play *You Can't Take It with You* gave him the opportunity to hone his comedy skills in an all-star cast. "I suppose it was a departure for me," he agreed, "and it gave me a bigger part with a certain amount of comedy."

The following year he won his first Oscar nomination as the idealistic young politician who takes on the establishment and its power-hungry members in *Mr. Smith Goes to Washington*. No movie fan will ever forget his filibuster and collapse on the floor of the senate.

"I won't forget it either," he said with a smile, "it took about ten days to shoot the whole scene. Frank had it covered with four cameras from different angles and distances. Then when he was ready for the close-up of me collapsing, he said, 'Now you've been working on this for some time, now do this one right, because this is the one we're going to use.' He always sensed the moment when everything was right for the final take."

The master of suspense, Alfred Hitchcock, was another film maker he admired greatly. Hitchcock not only moved him in a different dramatic direction, but also had a profound effect on his career. They collaborated on the suspense classics *Rope, Rear Window, The Man Who Knew Too Much* and *Vertigo*. "All the pictures he made are ageless and will be shown for years to come."

In 1935 the Stewart name first appeared on screen credits in a long-forgotten MGM drama starring Spencer Tracy, *The Murder Man*. The following year he appeared as Jeannette McDonald's fugitive brother, pursued by Mountie Nelson Eddy, in the well-remembered film treatment of *Rose Marie*. By 1937 he had graduated from Metro contract player to star billing in a re-make of *Seventh Heaven* opposite the French actress Simone Simon.

During his high school and college days he played the accordion for fun and profit and appeared in plays and musicals. In 1936 he was privileged to introduce, on a film soundtrack, one of Cole Porter's beguiling and enduring ballads. He sang it in a pleasing tenor voice. "Easy to Love" was written by the incomparable composer for the MGM movie *Born to Dance,* starring one of the screen's acclaimed dancers, Eleanor Powell. In order to win the male lead, he had to visit Porter's home and perform the song for the great man of music.

"I did audition for Cole Porter," Stewart recalled, as we reminisced in the den of his home on Roxbury Drive in Beverly Hills. "I remember it well—I was scared to death. I went to his house which was near the Beverly Hills Hotel and he was at the piano when I arrived. I knew the words but the melody was too high for my limited range. However, I sang it for him and he asked me to sing it again. Then I said something to him that I realized later you don't say to a famous composer, 'Would it be possible to change the key and bring it down to my level?' For a moment I thought they might change the actor instead, but they didn't—and they didn't change the key.

"A few days later, I pre-recorded the song for the soundtrack and nobody said anything about it. Then I went to the preview of the film, which was a nice movie and Eleanor Powell was great, but when it came to the scene for the song, I was quite surprised to hear another voice singing my song—it wasn't me! The studio had substituted a trained vocalist, who had a slight English accent, in my place.

"Although it is common Hollywood practice to have professional singers record soundtracks for actors, who then mouth the songs, it was nevertheless a discouraging moment for me. Years later I found out that following the preview the studio department heads decided that the song was so great that even my rendition couldn't hurt its popularity—so my voice was put back on the film soundtrack."

Few characterizations have impacted on the public's imagination like his charming performance as Elwood P. Dowd, the simple-minded young man who befriends an imaginary giant rabbit in the whimsical comedy *Harvey*.

He told me how he separated reality from fantasy in dealing with one of his favorite screen and stage roles.

"I never argued with myself about whether or not *Harvey* was a real person. He was just there as part of my subconscious. People ask me about that picture all the time. Once in a while when I travel, someone will come up to me on the street or at a gathering, and ask if Harvey is with me. I try to tell them politely that he couldn't make the trip, that he has a cold or is just under the weather, and had to stay home. They always reply by asking me to give him their best regards. I don't want to suggest that all of them are a little tipsy, some of them are just friendly, simple souls like Elwood P. Dowd, and I respect their vivid imaginations and am happy to commiserate with them."

His grandfather, James Maitland Stewart, opened a hardware store in Indiana, Pennsylvania, in 1853, where his family of Scottish-Irish ancestry had settled, and after military service, returned from the U.S. Civil War to resume its management. His son, Alexander (a World War I veteran), carried on the family business, married a local girl and raised a family of one son, James Maitland Stewart II, born May 20, 1908, and two daughters, Mary and Virginia.

Young Jimmy led an active, happy childhood and after high school graduation entered Princeton University, where he majored in architecture, winning a bachelor of science degree. During that time he became interested in acting. A schoolmate, who became a famous Broadway director and dramatist, Joshua Logan, formed the University

Players, which included Stewart and two of his future co-stars, Margaret Sullivan and Henry Fonda. A few years later, he and Fonda were struggling actors and roommates in New York.

No one in or out of show business was a closer friend than the late Henry Fonda. "It was a wonderful friendship all through our lives. There were times when we wouldn't see one another for a long time. He would be on tour with a play and I might be on location with a movie, but when we met again we would just pick up where we left off, which I think is a real sign of friendship." One topic that they never discussed was politics, since they had very different views. "We talked for about five minutes once about our political philosophies and we got into a fight, so we had a drink and agreed never to mention politics to one another again—and we didn't." They did make three films together, *On Our Merry Way* in 1948, *Firecreek* 20 years later, and *Cheyenne Social Club* in 1969.

Both men served their country in World War II, Fonda in the navy and Stewart in the air force. An enthusiastic flyer, he had a commercial pilot's license and volunteered for service. Underweight, he added extra pounds by eating bread and bananas, and was accepted. He became one of Hollywood's genuine war heroes. As commander of a B-24 squadron in England he rose to the rank of Lieutenant-Colonel and flew 20 bombing missions over enemy targets. One of the members of his squadron was a young actor named Walter Matthau. Colonel Stewart won the Air Force medal, the Croix de Guerre and the Distinguished Flying Cross. He retired from the air force reserve with the rank of Brigadier General.

Flying was one of the great passions of his life, and when it was announced in 1957 that Billy Wilder would bring to the screen the historic transatlantic flight of Charles Lindbergh, he campaigned for the role, even though he was too old for the part. But his youthful appearance and his superb performance made *The Spirit of St. Louis* a film triumph. "I really wanted the part," he told me, "because Lindbergh was always a hero to me. I knew I was too old, but I just didn't let it bother me and with makeup I was made to look younger."

In 1954 James Stewart was one of the screen's top stars; his popularity at the box office had never been higher. It was appropriate that the former Colonel Stewart of the U.S. Air Force should appear that year as Major Glenn Miller, the outstanding musician of World War II. *The Glenn Miller Story,* with June Allyson, was certainly one of his favorite films, but it was a challenge playing a well-remembered personality.

"Well, the trombone was the big problem. I was lucky to have an old friend who was an excellent trombonist and a veteran of the big band years, Joe Yukel, as my instructor. He not only demonstrated to me how I should simulate playing the instrument in the picture, but offered to give me lessons on the trombone. But after about a week of instructions and rehearsals he told me he was going to cancel the lessons. I was at a loss for words and asked him why he was quitting. He regretfully told me that the sounds I made trying to blow into the trombone had a terrible effect upon him. He said, 'I find myself going home after our rehearsals, and yelling at my wife and kids; I even kicked my dog, and I love my family and am very fond of my dog. I can't sleep at night!' So he said he had to quit, but he wished me good luck. Well, I made one of the quickest decisions of my life, and asked him if it would eliminate his problem if we put a plug in the mouthpiece, so it would be impossible for me to make any disturbing noises. He agreed, and then went on to teach me only the correct movements of the slide on the trombone, and it worked out pretty good. I was determined to have the movements correct, so no trombone player could later fault me for faking the playing."

For an eastern boy, a graduate of Princeton University, it was an amazing accomplishment that he should become one of the screen's top western stars. Directed by John Ford and Anthony Mann, his sagebrush classics included *The Man Who Shot Liberty Valance*, *The Far Country, Winchester '73*, *Broken Arrow* and his own favorite western, *The Man from Laramie*. He first rode the screen trails as a mild-mannered sheriff in *Destry Rides Again* opposite Marlene Dietrich.

Considered for many years as one of Hollywood's most eligible bachelors, he was 41 when he married the lovely model Gloria Hatrick McLean in 1949. He gained two sons by his wife's previous marriage: Ronald, who was killed in action in Vietnam, and his younger brother Michael. The Stewarts became parents of twin girls, Judy and Kelly, and proud grandparents. By the time of Gloria's death at the age of 75 in 1994, they had long been considered the movie colony's ideal couple. Their close friend, former President Ronald Reagan, said, "She was a very special woman with a wonderful sense of humor and not an ounce of self-pity."

As one of the screen's most versatile actors, Stewart won Hollywood's highest accolade early in his career, when he appeared opposite Katherine Hepburn and Cary Grant in *The Philadelphia Story*. His 1940 Oscar had a place of honor for years in his father's store: "Yes, it was there for 20 years in the window of the hardware store. My father always called me at about 4:00 in the morning—he never got on to the idea of the difference in the time zones. The morning after the Academy Awards I wasn't in a very good condition, after a late night of celebrating, when he called to tell me he had heard on the radio that I had won some kind of prize. He wanted to know what it was, and when I told him, he said 'Well, you better send it back and I'll put it in the window'—and I did and it was there for 20 years!"

In 1983 Indiana, Pennsylvania paid tribute to their favorite son with the unveiling of a statue of his likeness, near the location of his father's hardware store. "That was the place," he recalled fondly, "where I learned the value of hard work, the importance of community spirit, and the importance of family and faith in God. It's been a wonderful life. I've been fortunate and I'm grateful for every minute of it."

There is an old saying that you can't take the small town out of a small-town boy, and that saying, I believe, captures a great deal of the charm of Jimmy Stewart.

A tourist visits Rich Little and Jimmy Stewart during a break in the taping of a Dean Martin Roast, Las Vegas, February 1980.

"The Man Whose Name Was Far Above the Title." Academy Award-winning director Frank Capra at his estate in La Quinta, California, February 1980.

His Name Was Far Above the Title

Frank Capra's name was synonymous with the dreams and aspirations of the generation that endured the Great Depression of the 1930s. His memorable films emphasized the dignity of the average man and woman, who were victimized by a dehumanizing political era, but never lost hope in the face of despair.

When Gary Cooper appeared in *Meet John Doe* in 1941, Capra defined his optimistic approach to life. His inspiring family classic, *It's a Wonderful Life*, starring Jimmy Stewart, was a testament to his firm belief that there is inherent good in every person, and that every life influences the outcome of other lives. His philosophy for movie making was summed up in a simple statement: "What interests people most is people! An audience must be involved in the lives of screen characters, otherwise you won't have a believable or appealing story."

There is general agreement among film historians that Frank Capra's autobiography, *The Name Above the Title*, is the definitive book about the movies and Hollywood's golden years. In 1980 I was fortunate to be invited by the renowned director to his home in La Quinta, California.

He was six years old, the youngest of seven children, when the Capra family arrived in the United States from Sicily. They settled in the Los Angeles area, where his father worked in the area vineyards. Raised in the midst of ghetto poverty, he sought escape through education. He worked his way through university and graduated in 1918 as a chemical engineer at the California Institute of Technology. After service in the U.S. Army he was a mathematics teacher in San Francisco before he "backed into the movie business." His story reads like a Horatio Alger novel, or the script of one of his movies—a rags-to-riches wonderful life.

That remarkable life ended September 3, 1991. Two years earlier the American Film Institute honored him with their Lifetime Achievement Award. His death at 94 followed several years of failing health. His second wife, Lucille, died in 1984 after 52 years of marriage. She was a gracious hostess the day we visited their home near Palm Springs. Their eldest son, Tom, was the executive producer of NBC's *Today Show*. He has a sister and brother who bear their parents' names.

The winner of three Oscars as best director for *It Happened One Night*, *Mr. Deeds Goes to Town* and *You Can't Take It with You,* he began working in pictures only as a means of making a living. "My career was going to be in science," he told me. "I had no interest in films. I met a group of people who were investing in a new movie company. Like myself they had never been inside a studio, but I was younger and bolder than they were, and when I told them I was from Hollywood they opened their doors wide. I was broke at the time and needed work—and that's how I got into pictures."

Young Mr. Capra eventually came to the attention of the famous producers of two-reel comedies, Mack Sennett and Hal Roach. "They were the two busiest lots in Hollywood during the silents and early talkies," he recalled. "They both capitalized on name performers, but Sennett, who made his own headliners, wouldn't pay them what they were worth once they became stars, so all the big comedians, including Charlie Chaplin, left him over money. He didn't believe in scripts and would make up the plot of a picture while it was being shot."

In 1928 Capra began his stormy relationship with the acrimonious boss of the fledgling Columbia Pictures, Harry Cohn. They were constantly at odds over artistic control. "He was a dictator who oddly enough only admired people who refused to submit to his demands." A series of box-office and critically acclaimed Capra films established Columbia as a major studio.

It was during that period that the "talkies" were born, and movie makers and actors had to overcome severe technical problems to produce their sound pictures. "The microphones were all over the set," he recalled, "but they were hidden—they were in drawers, flower pots, anywhere out of sight. The actors had to talk right into them or they wouldn't be heard; so in the early days of the talkies a character would emote into one hidden mike and then move on to the next one. The cameras were placed in soundproof booths with little ventilation, so the cameraman could only shoot for a few minutes at a time. It was the best we could do.

"Many of the silent screen actors were terrified by the technical process and never made the transition to sound. They were used to working with a lot of noise. The quiet atmosphere of talking pictures and hearing only their own voices, coupled with memorizing lines, traumatized them. Stage actors flocked to Hollywood but also had difficulty coping with conditions on those early sound stages, where the heat generated by the equipment made working conditions unbearable."

At the 1933 Academy Awards dinner, Capra and his Columbia associates were ecstatic that one of his films, *Lady for a Day*, starring May Robson, had been nominated for four Oscars. It was the studio's first nominations. When emcee Will Rogers announced the name of the winning director, he said simply and warmly, "Come and get it, Frank!" The Columbia table exploded with applause, while Capra walked toward the dais, only to discover to his great embarrassment that the winner was Frank Lloyd for the epic feature *Cavalcade*.

Lady for a Day began a chain of 11 consecutive hits for the immigrant boy from Italy, and was followed in 1934 by the first movie to win five major Academy Awards, *It Happened One Night.*

"Best picture, actor, actress, writer and director, I got them all when I didn't expect to win. It was a sensational evening for all of us and especially Clark Gable. We had a lot of trouble casting, since light comedies do not read well. After several gals turned it down we couldn't find a guy to play the lead. We were going to call it off when Cohn got a call from the great Louis B. Mayer of MGM. He told us he had an actor who had been uncooperative and he wanted to loan him out as punishment for his behavior. So we got Clark Gable, who had been having contract problems at Metro, and a short time later Claudette Colbert, under similar circumstances—and that's how my most acclaimed film came about.

"Gable was anything but enthusiastic and came to us reluctantly. Columbia was the movie industry's Siberia, with its low budgets and inferior films. He was so annoyed and depressed that he arrived for our first meeting so drunk that he couldn't climb the steps to my office. But after a day or two of shooting he got into the part and he was a joy to work with—and I believe that was the only picture he made that he played himself. I'm sure that's why people found him so charming in that role. He was a very nice man and humble, who used to say, 'Well, they still haven't found me out!' He had no idea how good he was and couldn't handle the greatness that was thrust upon him, because he really didn't think he was that good an actor."

The Oscar-winning director who had a rare talent for blending scenes into appealing screen stories faced his most perplexing challenge when he adapted James Hilton's novel *Lost Horizon* to film. A magical movie of 1937 starring Ronald Colman, it almost bombed at the box office. During a sneak preview the audience broke into laughter during the opening sequence. What was supposed to be a serious scene sent a different signal to the first-nighter audience.

Capra, who was in the back of the theater during the disastrous preview, was humiliated and embarrassed. "We thought we had the loveliest picture ever made," he recalled, "so following the preview I went back to the projection room and thought over every scene in my mind.

Before long I realized that the opening, with its vignettes of everyday Oriental life, didn't fit the mood of the story. So I eliminated the first two reels, which were scene setters, and went right to the third reel where the action began. At the next screening there was no laughter in the wrong places. Editing changed the laughs to applause."

Despite the uncertain reaction of audiences, he was always opposed to private screenings. "Without an audience you have no film; they are a natural extension of the movie, the third dimension. Pictures are not made to be viewed alone in a projection room—the audience should influence the critic."

During the course of our lengthy interview he gave an intriguing analysis of the personalities and acting styles of the famous stars who appeared in his memorable films. Then he made a well-known observation, "You can be a star without being a good actor. Star quality is an indefinable quality that we recognize immediately. Many a millionaire has gone broke trying to make someone a star—but you've got to be born with it, whatever it is."

Two actors who radiated star quality appeared in five of the most successful Capra films: Gary Cooper starred in *Mr. Deeds Goes to Town* and *Meet John Doe,* and Jimmy Stewart headed the casts of *You Can't Take It with You*, *Mr. Smith Goes to Washington* and *It's a Wonderful Life*. While Cooper's career began a decade earlier than Stewart's, the two tall, lanky actors who were close friends were attracted to similar parts and had similar personalities.

"They were similar in naturalness but Stewart was versatile and could play any role; Cooper was not as pliable. But Gary had a face like Jimmy's that reflected honesty. He couldn't look bad, he was Mr. Integrity himself and always had that great quality of being believable. However, there were some parts he couldn't play. He might have been acceptable in *Mr. Smith Goes to Washington*, but then I thought I don't think he knows too much about Jefferson, Lincoln and Thomas Paine. I just didn't think he would be that comfortable with political history, so I thought I'd better get somebody who looks like they've been to school."

Capra had a sixth sense in getting exceptional work out of his actors. "It's the director's business to know how to coax the best performance out of a person," he emphasized, "and there are many ways to do it."

One of the most unusual Capra film sequences took place in the 1951 comedy *Here Comes the Groom*, which starred Bing Crosby and Jane Wyman. The action required the two stars to sing and dance through a lengthy production number that was shot on location in an office complex, went on to an elevator, descended a flight of stairs and emerged onto the street. A great admirer of Crosby, he knew that Bing liked to improvise as the cameras rolled. So rather than pre-record the song he decided to have the lengthy musical number performed live—which was unheard-of in movie-making circles.

"With Crosby, as he went along he thought of things to do. If you pre-recorded you locked him into the scene and he wasn't free to interpret his role. He was fantastic as he put in gags, little bits of business and ad-libbed a couple of lines in the song. When I found out that Jane Wyman could sing I realized I had to have a duet for them and found 'In the Cool, Cool, Cool of the Evening' on the shelf at Paramount. It had been written years before by Johnny Mercer and Hoagy Carmichael for a project that fell through, and went on to win the Academy Award for 1951 in our picture."

He once wrote that Bing Crosby did with his voice what he was doing on film, reflecting the dreams and aspirations of the people of his time—he referred to him as the Voice of America. It wasn't until the 1950s that they worked together, when Bing starred in two of his romantic comedies, *Riding High* and *Here Comes the Groom.* He felt that Bing's acting ability was underestimated and that he was without question the screen's most versatile performer.

"You could do things with Crosby that you couldn't do with anyone else; coordination, my goodness, he could juggle balls and play scenes at the same time—unlike most actors who can only do one thing at a time. He was the most un-actorish actor. One must never underestimate that it took great talent to do what he was doing. A tremendously talented man in singing, acting, performing—he was truly irreplaceable. He was so easy and wonderful to get along with, so able. Everybody knew he was the best popular singer ever, but he was also an outstanding actor—he could make you cry, make you laugh."

In 1959, toward the end of his career, Capra made his last critically acclaimed picture, featuring Frank Sinatra and Edward G. Robinson, *A*

Hole in the Head. It was a challenge for him to keep harmony on the set since his two actors came from different schools of acting.

"Sinatra, when he was in the mood, was a brilliant actor, but he would balk at doing a scene a second or third time. He never sang the same song in his concerts twice—if he could avoid an encore. If we had to shoot a scene over he could become very hard to handle. Barbara Stanwych was the same way. You had to get both of them on the first take or their performances would go downhill. On the other hand, Robinson liked to do a scene over and over getting better each time. When he couldn't have a lengthy rehearsal on the picture he'd get annoyed, especially if he thought I was giving in to Sinatra. He'd say, 'Oh you're afraid of him, he's got you bullied. Actors all get better as they rehearse!' And I'd reply, no they don't—some do, some don't."

Of all the actors who appeared in Capra movies, Jimmy Stewart was unquestionably his all-time favorite: "He's more than an actor, he's a human being on the screen; there are many actors who play parts well, but when you see him on the screen you don't see an actor. He's above acting and that's what makes him so appealing.

"It's like he's never read those lines before, it's 'now'; whatever is happening to him is now—for the first time. Nothing rehearsed, you don't see the machinery at all when he does his work and that's his great forte. He makes you feel that what he is thinking, saying and doing he just thought of it that moment. He had that quality from the beginning—all he needed was a good part to play. Very early, I learned to leave him alone and didn't try to change his style in any shape or manner; I'd just try to give him an idea of what the part was about."

At home with the "King of Swing" Benny Goodman, at his Manhattan penthouse apartment, September 30, 1979.

The King of Swing

Benny Goodman was the undisputed "King of Swing." He played a unique and decisive role in the development of the Big Band Era. As a musician he had no equal; he was as much at home in a concert hall as he was on a bandstand. In an unprecedented career that spanned more than six decades, he was internationally acclaimed as both a popular and a classical clarinet virtuoso.

In 1938 he made a major contribution in establishing jazz as an art form with his Carnegie Hall concert. That same year he made his classical debut with the Budapest String Quartet.

As a committed advocate of racial equality, at a time when even dance bands were segregated in the United States, he hired a promising black vibraphonist, the brilliant Lionel Hampton, who went on to lead his own orchestra.

Prior to a 1979 Goodman tour I met with him on an autumn afternoon at his New York penthouse apartment. Although he had a reputation among musicians as a demanding taskmaster, he was most cordial and quite charming during our lengthy interview. Soft-spoken and disarming, he recalled the events and people that contributed to his success.

Born May 30, 1909, he was the eighth of eleven children of an immigrant couple who settled in Chicago. At the synagogue that his family attended he began his musical education. "One of my brothers was given a trombone," he recalled, "another brother received a trumpet, and I guess because I was the smallest, they gave me an E-flat clarinet. I was about nine years old."

His father was a tailor who made every effort to pass on his love of music to his children. "My Dad worked very hard and made many sacrifices to get us private lessons, which cost about 35 cents an hour in those days. I don't believe he thought it would be a profession for us, but he hoped it would have a good influence on us."

The Goodman saga began with his joining a local jazz band that played around the Chicago area. "I probably was only 12 or 13 when I first got paid as a musician," he told me. By 1926 he was a member of the Ben Pollack Band, playing both saxophone and clarinet. "Back then every member of the orchestra had to double on a variety of instruments. It was at that time that I did my first solo work on a recording of 'Deed I Do.'

"I was about sixteen when I went out to California with Pollack, and it was then that Glenn Miller joined the band. We were roommates and became pals, hanging out together, double-dating and so forth. Glenn was a very keen musician, but to be honest he had trouble playing the trombone, as compared to the likes of Jack Teagarden. But he made up for it in other ways—as an arranger he was always full of ideas and he developed the most identifiable sound of all the big bands."

A few years later, they were both playing in the pit orchestra for the Gershwin Broadway hit *Girl Crazy*. Gene Krupa was the drummer.

By 1934, with his own band, Goodman made his network radio debut. "It was really the forerunner of a lot of radio programs, including the *Lucky Strike Hit Parade*. There were three bands on the show:

Xavier Cugat played Latin melodies, Cal Murray headed a full orchestra and we were the jazz band. Prior to that we were at Billy Rose's Music Hall, where we got excellent reviews, and were asked to audition for what was then called the *National Biscuit Program*. The show was broadcast live, for both the east and the west, so we would spend hours in the studio rehearsing and performing."

No one was more closely associated with the word "swing" than the man who brought that style of music to the Big Band Era. "Well, we used to use that term all the time, but I didn't think of using it as a means of identification, until a publicist arranging our first tour wanted to identify the band with the kind of music we played. And it was Gene Krupa who said, 'Benny, why don't you call it a swing orchestra—that's what we play,' and I think I said, 'that's good, let's leave it that way.'"

Goodman's ear for talent launched the careers of an impressive group of performers including Harry James, Peggy Lee, Teddy Wilson and the aforementioned Messrs. Krupa and Hampton. With his trios, quartets, quintets and sextets, he featured exceptional musicians from the world of jazz, like Canada'a Peter Appleyard, and set musical standards that were beyond compare.

I was curious whether his familiar theme, "Let's Dance," came out of his radio program, or whether it was written before he began his broadcasts. "I've never been asked that before," was his surprising answer. "It wasn't my idea," he continued. "A friend of mine, Joseph Bonine, thought the lovely classical piece 'Invitation to the Dance,' could be adapted to a dance beat, and we had George Baskin make an arrangement of it and we took it as our theme. It was probably after our early broadcasts." It was Gordon Jenkins who wrote the Goodman sign-off theme, the appropriate, "Goodbye."

In 1955 Steve Allen starred in *The Benny Goodman Story*, a film that brought his private as well as his public life into focus. He and his wife Alice were married in 1942 and had two children, Rachel and Benjie. The highlight of the movie was the Carnegie Hall concert of 1938, which was the musical milestone of his outstanding career. "I guess it was quite a momentous occasion," he agreed, "although we didn't think so at the time. It was a press agent's idea. We thought it was a rather silly proposition and couldn't imagine why we would want to play there. Sometimes you are kind of goaded into doing something, and we finally decided somewhat reluctantly to do it, and I guess you could say the rest is history."

Toward the end of his career he traveled extensively for the U.S. State Department as a goodwill ambassador, and gave concerts for worthy causes around the world.

Following a lengthy illness, Benny Goodman passed away in 1986, only a few months after he had attended the recording industry's Grammy Awards, where his fellow musicians and admiring fans presented him with an honor that was long overdue, their Lifetime Achievement Award.

✪ ✪ ✪

...ANECDOTE

Nothing is more disconcerting to an actor than to look out at an audience and notice someone nodding off. It's an occupational hazard that even radio interviewers can experience. In a spacious hotel lobby I once interviewed the delightful English actor and music hall performer, Stanley Holloway. It was a major remote broadcast with impressive looking equipment, miles of wires and my personal radio technicians. As I began the interview a man walked in front of us and sat down on a sofa immediately across from where we were sitting. He began to read his newspaper and was oblivious to our radio broadcast. Before we had concluded what was for me a fascinating conversation, the paper fell from his hands and on to the floor as he fell sound asleep. He then began to snore loudly. Mr. Holloway looked at me and said: "Well, we certainly kept his interest, didn't we? I've had that happen on the stage but never during an interview."

One of my most interesting interviews took place in June 1984 when Raymond Burr visited Ottawa.

The Courtroom Was His Sound Stage

Whenever long-time TV viewers reminisce about the most memorable dramatic series on television, one name is certain to be mentioned, Raymond Burr, the star of two video classics, the Emmy award winners *Perry Mason* and *Ironside*.

At six foot three, with a robust frame and commanding presence, and blessed with a deep warm voice, the dominant actor of TV courtroom dramas was a striking figure on or off the screen. He was also one of the friendliest and most convivial actors that I have had the pleasure of interviewing.

In 1984 he revived his characterization as Perry Mason for a TV movie that brought him and his most famous role out of retirement. *The Return of Perry Mason* topped the ratings and was so well received by the critics and public that two or three Mason movies were filmed every year thereafter until his death from cancer in 1993. The only surviving member of the original company, Barbara Hale, appeared as his faithful secretary, Della Street, in every show. The original one-hour weekly courtroom drama series, based on Erle Stanley Gardner's creation, ran from 1957 to 1966 and produced an amazing 283 episodes. The demanding shooting schedule made him a virtual prisoner of the popular format for over nine years.

"I had no time to get around in public," he told me. "I lived in the studio and stayed there six days a week, driving from Hollywood to my home in Malibu late Saturday night for Sunday at the house.

"In retrospect I don't think the programs would have been as successful without that kind of commitment. It came, however, at a time in my life when I was young, when I should have been married with a family and done all the things that any normal person does in the pursuit of life, love and happiness. I had none of those opportunities for nearly a decade. I am glad, of course, that I did the show, but I am sorry that I did it every week for as long as I did."

When the Mason series was being planned several actors auditioned for the starring role, including major stars like Fred MacMurray, but strangely enough Burr was asked to do a screen test for the part of the prosecuting attorney, Hamilton Burger. "I told them I would only do the test," he recalled, "if I was also allowed to audition for the part of Mason. I wasn't interested in doing another prosecuting attorney, after appearing in that role in three movies, so they agreed—and Erle saw both my tests and apparently I was what he was looking for in his famous fictional character."

Erle Stanley Gardner died in 1981 at age 85. Legend has it that when he saw the Burr auditions he said emphatically, "That's him! That's Perry Mason!" The two men became both business associates and friends. "We weren't that close in the early years, but as we grew older we became very good friends."

The original series, filmed in black and white, continues to attract old and new audiences in reruns around the world, which was a comfort to him when he thought back to the exhausting schedule he endured. "I got up every morning at five and worked on my lines throughout the day. Mason, of course, had a monstrous amount of dialogue in every script, so there was just no way out of the studio and that's why I had to live in my dressing room. The actual filming would take place in the evening, and it was always very tiring, both physically and emotionally.

"I'll tell you a true story," he continued. "It happened in the seventh year of the series. One day I decided I just had to get outdoors and get a little fresh air. I went for a walk throughout the area and discovered a 12-story office building that wasn't there when we began shooting earlier in the year. I spent so much time in the studio that I hadn't seen it before. It was at that time that I started thinking seriously about getting out of the weekly TV grind."

In the eyes of many TV viewers Raymond Burr was the incomparable courtroom lawyer Perry Mason or the dedicated police chief Robert Ironside. They found it difficult at times to separate his private life from his famous fictional roles. "Especially in the early years of Mason," he remembered, "when people would stop me on the street wondering if I could help them with a legal problem. I eventually had to set up a service in my office to put these viewers in touch with legal aid groups and attorneys that I could recommend to them. People thought I was so much into the law that I could really do something for them."

Although he lived most of his life in California his roots were deep in Canada. He was born in New Westminster, B.C., in 1917. His father, who passed away at 98, lived on Canada's west coast. A sister and late brother were also residents of B.C.

Long before his television stardom the name Burr was included in major radio, TV and movie credits. He was in demand as a character actor from the time of his arrival in Hollywood. He played a variety of roles, from villains to lawyers and detectives.

Young Raymond was only 12 years old when he made both his theater and radio debut in San Francisco, where his family lived for several years. As a young adult in New York he was a radio newscaster by day and a stage actor by night. His resonant voice made him a natural news reader, until one day he decided he'd better pursue another career. "Gordon, I've never told this story publicly. It was around 1936 at the time of Hitler's rise to power. I read the first item on a fifteen-minute newscast and suffered my first major blooper when I tried to say with authority, 'the peace treaties' and said instead 'the trease peeties,' and then repeated the same words three times without getting them right. After that goof, I guess I lost my self-confidence and never did a bit of news from that day forward."

As an actor his radio credits were staggering. "I did, including shows for the armed forces, over 5000 programs. I was very fortunate in my younger years to become part of that inner circle that was in Hollywood at that time. We would rehearse one show, go to another studio for a live broadcast and sometimes do three broadcasts in one day. I did mostly dramatic shows. I worked with Lionel Barrymore on his radio program, which was a joy to do, and also with John and Ethel Barrymore on radio dramas. I did Jack Webb's shows, *Pete Kelly's Blues* and *Dragnet*. I was on the first TV presentation of *Dragnet* as the Chief of Detectives."

Burr's name was linked not only to the stars of the past but to many of today's reigning celebrities. "The TV syndicators had a great promo for the reruns of the old black and white Mason programs to attract younger viewers: 'You never know who you will see on *Perry Mason*'; then they would show photos of Robert Redford, Burt Reynolds, Jack Nicholson and almost everyone who is a major star today. They were all on the Mason show at one time or another."

Long before his television notoriety he was a very busy film actor. One of his most memorable supporting roles was as the villain in the 1954 thriller *Rear Window*. "Alfred Hitchcock and I became great friends. I went to Europe while *Rear Window* was still playing and discovered that character actors were given greater prominence there than in North America. Wherever I traveled in Europe I found myself sharing the billing with the film's two stars, Jimmy Stewart and Grace Kelly. I did several interviews and was almost always introduced as being Raymond Burr in Alfred Hitchcock's *Rear Window*.

"When I eventually went to Universal to work I was surprised and pleased that my dressing room was right next to the Hitchcock complex. My kitchen looked out at his front door. So, as a prank, I had a big cutout made of him and put it in the kitchen window with a hand coming around the shutters. I lit it properly and it really looked like Mr. Hitchcock was standing in the window. Then, when tour guides went by I had them say to their tour groups, 'Oh! There's Alfred Hitchcock in Raymond Burr's rear window.' He put up with it for about six months and then sent me a note saying, 'Dear Raymond, six months is enough.' So I took it down in hopes that I would work with him again. But I think he did enjoy my gag and the turn of phrase."

The second acclaimed Raymond Burr TV series, *Ironside*, in which he portrayed a disabled police chief who fought crime from a wheelchair, was on the air for eight years, from 1967 to 1975. "I wasn't going to do another series," he admitted, "because the thinking around Hollywood was that I was too closely associated with Mason to do another character. I first did *Ironside* as a TV movie and it was an instant ratings hit and led to a very successful run. While it emphasized the need for good police work in a violent society, it did it with compassion. From the beginning we thought that the character could be a positive role model—and we were proud to have played an important part in advancing the laws to improve the lifestyle of the handicapped."

Despite his busy TV schedule he was attracted to the stage and was considering a play that he would eventually take to Broadway. It was a new play by Jay Broad with the working title *A Conflict of Interest.* I was surprised when he sent me a copy of the script and asked me if I thought it would be well received by Canadian audiences. It is now a treasured remembrance of an exceptional actor and a good friend.

With considerable financial holdings in Canada, he was pleased to film the Mason TV movies in Vancouver and Toronto. Over lunch, during one of his visits to Ottawa, he took great delight in regaling us with anecdotes and special memories of his happy childhood in British Columbia.

His most satisfying accomplishment was being inducted into the "TV Hall of Fame"—which was an appropriate gesture from an industry that recognizes its pioneers and renowned figures.

Despite being diagnosed in 1991 with cancer of the kidney, Raymond Burr insisted on leading a full productive life as long as he could. Only months before his death he went before the cameras in an

Ironside Reunion movie and a final Perry Mason film, *The Case of the Killer Kiss*, which was the 26th episode since he had brought the fabled lawyer back to TV. He bequeathed most of his considerable wealth to charities and insisted on keeping up a busy schedule in fund-raising so that "no one would be disappointed."

His final days were spent at his Sonoma County, California farm where he succumbed to the deadly disease with dignity and forbearance. He was a big man in every way and bravely faced his greatest adversary privately, not wishing to burden and distress his many friends. He left his close associates and innumerable fans September 12, 1993.

Raymond Burr was so closely associated with Perry Mason that people asked him for legal advice. We met again in the fall of 1986.

"I would rather have been a flop in show business than a success in something else." George Burns at his Hollywood office, January 21, 1976.

The Last of the Sunshine Boys

George Burns was a show business phenomenon. His success as a performer was unequalled. In contrast to other entertainers he became more popular as he grew older. When he was well into his nineties he was still a headliner. Only failing health brought his unique career to an end.

He was unable to celebrate his 100th birthday, January 20, 1996, on stage in Las Vegas as he had planned, but it was observed by the industry he loved with greetings and warm tributes from his countless friends and fans. His death a short time later was mourned around the world.

Back in 1976, at the time of our first meeting, he was quick to dismiss the thought of retirement: "I don't think anyone should retire," he said with conviction. His meaning was clear, that no one should retire from life. The interview took place the day after his 80th birthday at his Hollywood office in General Studios, which was near the sound stage where he and his late wife, Gracie Allen, filmed their long-running TV series.

"The most important thing when you get to be my age," he continued, "is to have something to get you out of bed in the morning, something to look forward to, a deadline or a meeting with someone. Keep moving and try to look as good as you can for your age. If you are going to retire from your work, then retire to something—do something!" That advice is personally more relevant now than it was that wonderful morning I spent with the ageless philosopher of show business.

During our lengthy conversation, and during subsequent interviews, he recalled many amusing incidents and old friends.

"I was a late bloomer," he said with a twinkle in his eyes. "I never knew I was an actor until I was 79 and did *The Sunshine Boys*. I was 33 when I made my first movie, but had to wait until I was 80 to win an Oscar. Then I went to Nashville, and after singing all my life found out at 84 that I was a recording star with a hit record."

On Manhattan's lower east side, where he was born the ninth of twelve children, the Burns love affair with show business began. As a member of a neighborhood vocal group, The Peewee Quartet, he sang and danced on the streets of New York to help support his family. He was a vaudeville veteran by the time he was 14. When he and an early partner, Abie Kaplan, stole chunks of coal from the Burns Brothers Coal Yard, Nathan Birnbaum became George Burns.

After years of seeing his name at the bottom of theatrical bills, he became a headliner when he met a pretty Irish colleen from San Francisco, who became his partner and the love of his life, Gracie Allen. Unlike some comedy teams they were a perfect blend both on and off stage. "It's true," he recalled, "that comedy partners often didn't get along. McIntyre & Heath were a popular vaudeville team that worked together for years but didn't talk to one another or mix socially. The acts where the talent was equally divided caused bouts of jealousy—like the characters Walter Matthau and I played in *The Sunshine Boys*. But it was never a problem for me, because our talent was about 90 to 10 percent in Gracie's favor."

Their lifelong friends were Jack and Mary Benny; Benny was Burns' best pal and favorite comedy foil. Everything that Burns said and did made Benny laugh uproariously. "We were in the Brown Derby once having lunch and Jack said, 'I don't like bread without butter and I'm on a diet and Mary said I shouldn't have butter.' So I said, 'Well, Mary isn't here, go ahead and have butter; I won't tell.' Then when the cheque arrived I told him to pay it or I would tell Mary that he had butter.

"Another time he said to me, 'I didn't sleep last night, but the night before I had a good sleep." So I got another big laugh out of him when I told him to sleep every other night. And then there was the time that we were at a party and I removed a thread from his jacket and said, 'I didn't know they were wearing them this year.' He fell down laughing. A few days later I mailed the thread back to him and thanked him for letting me borrow it. It was silly things like that that broke him up."

It was Rich Little who first put me in touch with one of his all-time favorite performers. His letter-perfect impression of the legendary comedian not only amazed Burns, but made him an instant Little fan. "He's the best I've ever heard—the greatest! He does me so well that sometimes I'm not sure if I'm George Burns or Rich Little. Every time he's on TV I'm so confused that I expect to be paid by the producer."

Upon hearing of his death, Rich said with sorrow and love, "As long as I perform, George will live on in my act. It's the best way I can keep his memory alive."

The Burns persona was so well defined that he was widely imitated and quoted. But he insisted that it is the public who are responsible for developing a performer's image. "You've got nothing to do with it—the audience does it for you. They decide how you will act and whether you will be a star or a flop. When Gracie and I began in vaudeville she would do a few wisecracks that I wrote and some silly questions. The audience laughed at the silly stuff, but they didn't like her being sarcastic. In the beginning, for just one show, our roles were reversed. She played straight, asking the questions, and I had the jokes and wore funny clothes. The people laughed at Gracie's questions, but nobody laughed at my answers."

In private life Burns and Allen were opposites in personalities and interests, just as they were in their well-remembered performances. "Gracie was not as enthusiastic about show business as I was. I'll never forget one time when I got great news about our show. Back then the TV networks would sign you for 40 weeks and 12 weeks of repeats. We had just been picked up by Carnation Milk and I ran home and said to her excitedly, 'Gracie, I've got some great news,' and she said, 'Not now, George, Ma Perkins is in trouble.' So I had to wait until the end of a soap opera to tell her that we had won the biggest contract of our career."

Their theme song, "The Love Nest," will linger on as long as there is show business, as will their familiar sign-off, "Say Goodnight, Gracie." "It was the most natural line to get off our show with, and years later they used it on *Laugh-In*." Then in typical Burns manner he said, "If you say something every week it gets to be a quotable line. Let me tell you something; if you are on a program every week, even if you have no talent you can get to be a personality. People will say, 'How do you like that, he's on every week and he has no talent!' Gracie had enough for both of us."

Contrary to his modest self-image, he had an overabundance of talent as a straight man, comedian, singer, hoofer, actor and best-selling author.

The 1976 Oscar he won for Best Supporting Actor opposite Walter Matthau in *The Sunshine Boys* brought him full circle in Hollywood. "I hadn't made a picture in 36 years, and I had never appeared in a film as anyone but myself. Appearing as an old vaudevillian, Al Lewis, was easy, because I've been a vaudeville 'Sunshine Boy' most of my life. My dear friend in heaven, Jack Benny, made a great test for the part, but took ill a short time later. When he left us I was asked to read for the part. It wasn't a challenge, because I knew the character well. I came from New York, and the way Neil Simon wrote his words they were a perfect fit for my mouth, because I've heard people talk that way all my life."

During the years that followed his film comeback his star shone brightly as he starred in box-office hits that included *Oh, God!* with John Denver; two sequels to that off-beat comedy; and the critically acclaimed *Going In Style*, with Art Carney and Lee Strasberg. His TV appearances were always well received. In 1980 he traveled to Nashville and recorded an album that remained on the charts for over a year—it included the nostalgic hit "I Wish I Was 18 Again." He always loved to sing, and was encouraged to vocalize by Gracie, who dubbed him "Sugarthroat Burns."

"When I first began performing I sang with a group of kids. Most people like to sing, but few have the courage that I have, because I don't care if people like my singing or not. Many of the songs I feature were popular when I was growing up. The audience accepts them even though they date back to the early part of the century."

By the time he was 92 the Burns name had made the best-seller lists several times in bookstores around the world. His 100th birthday inspired the last book he authored. One of his autobiographical reminiscences was lovingly entitled *Gracie: A Love Story*. It was a warm account of their lives together, from the time they met in vaudeville until her death in 1964. She was only 58 when she succumbed to heart disease. Their marriage of over four decades was as close-knit as their professional relationship. "I knew all about show business, but I didn't know how to do it—Gracie could do it, and that made us a very good combination. Gracie had natural talent, and all I did was ask her questions about her family, and she talked until her retirement 38 years later. I guess being with her all those years some of her talent had to rub off on me." Their familiar roles of the scatterbrain wife and nonplussed husband were developed almost by chance. "I noticed in the beginning that when our jokes were off-center, Gracie would get big laughs. The audience really did develop our characters and style.

"Since Gracie's personality was off-beat, we decided to make her relatives eccentric, because you couldn't have an intellectual family and get laughs. We even did a routine on radio that revolved around her brother being lost. She went from show to show looking for him. It was the first time anyone had walked into another program and the first time anyone had crossed networks with a running gag. It happens often now, but it caused quite a sensation back then. The amusing fact was that Gracie had a real brother, George Allen. He took such a ribbing from friends and strangers that he changed his name until the routine had run its course."

Young at heart, George Burns attributed his longevity to his love of life. "If you do things you enjoy," he told me, "I don't think you ever grow old." Then with a chuckle in his voice he added, "a diet of prunes and martinis also keeps you going."

As he approached his 100th birthday, the entertainment world's only centenarian star was as thrilled to hear the sound of applause as he was the first time he appeared before an audience.

When we first met he ended our interview with a statement that summed up his professional life: "I've said it many times before, and I'll say it again, I would rather have been a flop in show business than a success in something else. I love show business as much today as when I first started." And as far as his fans were concerned, the feeling was mutual. He was in every sense of the word a show business phenomenon.

✪ ✪ ✪

...ANECDOTE

Whenever someone would ask George Burns what his doctor thought of him smoking several cigars a day, he had a ready answer. He would take a long drag on his cigar, blow out perfect smoke rings at the questioner, and reply, "He's dead!"

Backstage with Frank Sinatra at the "million dollar Ottawa concert," September 1982. "It was vintage Sinatra!" (Photo by John Evans)

A Man Alone

"A Man Alone" is the title of one of Frank Sinatra's beautiful and highly emotional record collections. It would be an appropriate theme for a theatrical or film account of his life and times. A private person, he is sometimes described by his friends and associates as a mercurial man. The public image he projects is one of contradictions, of someone who is at different times controversial, compassionate, complex and colorful—and at all times a consummate entertainer, who will be remembered as one of the exceptional performers of the 20th century.

The dynamic balladeer, who has cast spells upon his audiences with his matchless phrasing, intensity and contrasting moods—and the finger-snapping swingin' song stylist, who has put audiences into orbit—began his career over five decades ago in his home town, Hoboken, New Jersey, during the bleak years of the Depression and the early days of World War II.

From his big band years to the September of his years, and from swoon crooner to show business legend, Frank Sinatra's career has been a fascinating blend of Horatio Alger and "What Makes Sammy Run."

Frank was an only child. His mother, Natalie, who was known to her friends as Dolly, was a caring ambitious lady, who had a profound effect upon him throughout his life. His father, Anthony, was a fireman who rose to the rank of captain.

With three friends, Frank formed a group called the Hoboken Four, who were winners on radio's *Original Amateur Hour*. His solo career began with the Harry James Band, which led to his formative years as featured vocalist with Tommy Dorsey.

After his swoon-crooner popularity of the 1940s subsided, he made an amazing show business comeback in 1954. A distinctive new sound arranged by Nelson Riddle was the musical foundation of his renewed popularity. Shortly before his passing, Nelson Riddle made this comment during one of my Hollywood interviews: "Some people say I was responsible for his comeback, but I always hoped that wouldn't reach his ears. If the association was good for him, it was also important for me."

Although Sinatra retired from show business in the early 1970s, he soon became restless from inactivity, and urged on by his fans, resumed his career.

In more recent years most of his travels have been on behalf of charitable causes. It was in the planning and preparation of such an event that I first met him. Rich Little had appeared with him at several fund-raising concerts and in return Sinatra had agreed to do a benefit performance in Rich's home town on behalf of the Ottawa Civic Hospital.

A short time later in Palm Springs, California, while on a radio assignment, my wife and I were privileged to visit the former Sinatra estate. The night before Rich had taken part in a high-priced benefit, arranged by Sinatra's wife Barbara, on behalf of a local hospital. Rich and his wife were weekend guests at the Sinatras' along with other celebrities who had taken part in the fund-raiser, Debby Boone, Peter Falk and the late arranger-conductor, Don Costa. (In 1994 the Sinatras sold their sumptuous estate for simpler surroundings and a more casual life style in Malibu, California.)

Upon our arrival at their desert complex, where we were to meet the

Littles and accompany them to their home in Malibu, we were invited to join the Sinatras and their guests for Sunday brunch. This unexpected invitation gave us a rare insight into the social graces the Sinatras extend to their friends and acquaintances. As strangers, who must have appeared a little uncomfortable in such high profile company, we were immediately put at ease by our famous hosts.

I had a delightful conversation with Sinatra about his boyhood idol Bing Crosby. He had heard excerpts from my Crosby radio anthology and seemed quite interested in the series and my long friendship with Bing. "How did you ever get Crosby to sit still so long?" he asked with a smile. "All those questions and anecdotes. He was my friend and I could never keep him from moving on. We might meet at a cocktail party, start talking, and when I would turn around to get my glass refilled, he'd be gone—like he went right through the wall. But then, he was never comfortable at cocktail parties." Then he added as a warm afterthought—"but he was a wonderful friend, and a great guy."

While we were talking, to our surprise, an old Crosby movie came on the screen of an overhead TV. We both thought it was an amusing coincidence.

During brunch he thoughtfully arranged for his guests to receive a personally autographed copy of his definitive album, *Trilogy*. It was to be released by Reprise Records a few days later, and the advance copies immediately became collector's items. Without asking, he autographed my collection, "To Gordon, Enjoy! Frank Sinatra." One of the songs from the set became one of his biggest hits, "New York, New York."

The Sinatra property was situated on a street named after him, and was encircled by a high fence that not only assured privacy to those inside, but hid the grounds from public view. Contrary to his media image of flamboyance and hostility, the atmosphere at his estate was inviting and hospitable. The guard at the gatehouse looked more like a friendly neighbor from Andy Griffith's *Mayberry* than a member of an entourage.

The residents of Palm Springs referred to the Sinatra estate as "The Compound." It was an accurate description, since there were several structures on the property, the main building being a one-story mansion that rambled across the grounds. We entered by a spacious recreation room where the brunch was taking place.

Barbara Sinatra graciously took us and the Littles on a tour of her beautiful home, where we admired her art collection and the many mementos of Sinatra's career, including his Oscar for his riveting supporting performance as Maggio in *From Here to Eternity*. We were surprised and intrigued to discover that he was a railroad buff with a most unusual collection of miniature trains, which included locomotives and railway cars as both hobby and art pieces. One of his prize possessions was a gold-plated model of an early western train. In the middle of the property there was an old restored caboose that he had remodeled as a sauna. Four guest cottages with individual swimming pools were within view of the main house. All the rooms throughout the estate were named after Sinatra hit songs, with one romantic ballad borrowed from his *High Society* co-star Bing, "True Love."

Back in the early 1960s when President Kennedy was expected as a house guest, a helicopter pad was put in place on the grounds of the estate, but the White House canceled the visit. The press suggested that Kennedy aides were concerned about alleged Sinatra connections with questionable associates.

Following brunch we thanked our hosts for their hospitality and made tentative plans for our Ottawa benefit concert. Sinatra was laughing loudly as we drove from the grounds, with Rich doing an impromptu *Columbo* for Peter Falk.

It is a measure of Sinatra the man that he can be very considerate when working with his friends. There is no better example of his generosity than his 1982 Ottawa concert with Rich. The evening raised a record-breaking one million dollars from a black tie dinner hosted by Prime Minister Trudeau, followed by a sell-out concert. Not only was the hospital's special care nursery, which was built from the money raised that night, named after Rich, but Frank insisted that he would go on first, so that Rich would close the show before his home-town fans.

It was vintage Sinatra that night and a concert that will long be remembered as one of his finest. In his introductory remarks he made the following considerate and revealing statement: "I want to take a moment to tell you that I am truly delighted to be a part of this evening, because it is most important. You know what it is all about and you are the heroes and heroines of the evening for lending your support, and I congratulate you. You have done a wonderful thing tonight. God bless you all for that.

"We hope you will enjoy the program. I tried to mix the songs up so that you will recognize most of them. Of course, you understand without my saying, that we don't do anything that is done by the guys with the funny suits and funky shoes, because I don't know how to do that stuff—I got to do what we do best." And with that lighthearted remark he began an almost flawless performance that was one of his biggest money-making concerts.

Despite the stormy chapters in *The Sinatra Story*, he has always been close to his three children, daughters Nancy and Tina and his only son, Frank. While the younger Frank pursued a singing career for several years in the 1980s, he joined his Dad full-time as his musical conductor. I met with the multi-talented younger Sinatra, who made this frank statement about his famous father: "That man you are speaking of, I am his son; everything I am he gave to me. I will never lock him out of my life professionally or personally. Professionally it hurts occasionally that I have to sacrifice some of my own identity to establish his; but still everything I have he gave me. The fact is, I must do his bidding for as many years as he is here, and long after he is gone. My father is my father—he has given me everything."

Of all the citations, awards, international acclaim and glowing reviews that Frank Sinatra has received throughout his career, a comment from his boyhood hero and musical mentor, Bing Crosby, is among his most meaningful and treasured statements. It was during one of my interviews with Bing that he had this to say about Sinatra the performer, and Frank, the man:

"I hold him in great respect. He is one of the few singers in my opinion who creates a mood when he sings. It's not just the song or what he says, it's an ambience or attitude—a mood is the best way to describe it—Nat Cole did that too. Frank really owns an audience when he starts singing; he has a tremendous command and can sing any kind of song that I can think of—he can handle it. He has great communication and talent. He is a remarkable person and an outstanding entertainer."

At Henry Mancini's office on Sunset Boulevard, July 1975. (I had to return the shirt to a jockey friend at Delmar Race Track!)

Mancini at the Movies

Henry Mancini, Hollywood's gifted and versatile composer, arranger and conductor, was one of the most popular and respected members of the music and movie fraternities. His early love of motion pictures never waned. "If I had only one thing to do," he once said, "I would want to write film scores. That's where it all started and that's where I'm most comfortable." In a manner of speaking, the industry he loved "skipped a beat" when he passed away June 14, 1994. He was survived by his wife of 47 years, Ginny, their son Chris and twin daughters Monica and Felice.

Two months earlier, on April 19, his 70th birthday was celebrated by 4000 friends and fans at a benefit concert in Los Angeles, where he was awarded a Lifetime Grammy Achievement Award. Julie Andrews and Andy Williams, who popularized his songs, headed an all-star cast.

Only a few weeks earlier he had been diagnosed as suffering from terminal pancreatic cancer. During his brief illness he continued to work on the arrangements for a Broadway adaptation of his score of *Victor/Victoria*, the 1982 film that starred Andrews and Robert Preston.

When I first met with him at his skyscraper office, located at the corner of Sunset and Vine in Hollywood, we were surrounded by keepsakes of his impressive career, which included a Pink Panther doll and his own pencil sketch of Peter Gunn.

Born in Cleveland, Ohio, Mancini was raised in Alquippa, Pennsylvania, the son of an immigrant couple. His father worked in the steel mills and played flute in the local Sons of Italy band. As a boy he was more interested in football than music, but he was persuaded by his parents to study piccolo, flute and piano. "When I discovered jazz," he told me, "I listened to fellas like Art Tatum and André Previn and I knew I couldn't play piano like that, and when I listened to classical pianists I knew I wasn't that good—so I think that threw me into writing." Nevertheless, his unique piano touch often highlighted his recordings and concerts. "I found a way to put my simple style to good use and I believe I developed a distinctive piano sound that sets a plaintive mood. The first time I recorded successfully at the piano was on the theme for *Romeo and Juliet* and that set the pace for my albums *A Warm Shade of Ivory* and *Love Story*."

There was a classical touch to many Mancini arrangements which he attributed to his years of serious study and training. "I had several excellent teachers," he recalled, "and attended both Carnegie and Julliard schools of music."

Mancini's accomplishments were truly amazing. He recorded 90 albums, received 72 Grammy nominations and was a winner 20 times. His scoring for films and original movie ballads garnered him 18 Academy Award nominations. He won Oscars in 1961 for *Breakfast at Tiffanys* and the song from that score, "Moon River." The following year he repeated for best song with "The Days of Wine and Roses" and 20 years later won his fourth Academy Award for *Victor/Victoria*. Other significant Mancini titles included "Whistling Away the Dark," Dear Heart," "Charade," "Sweetheart Tree" and "Baby Elephant Walk."

He never deviated from his format when scoring movies. "I don't begin a score until I have seen the film. I prefer it that way. I would rather get an impression as to what the picture needs, and what the flow of the story is, and then proceed to score."

He was only 18 when he joined the U.S. Air Force and was assigned to a band in Atlantic City. It was there that he met Glenn Miller, who was organizing musical aggregations for the Air Force. In 1944, with the Battle of the Bulge raging in Normandy, his group were all transferred to the army. "I've often thought," he said with a wry smile, "how desperate the Allies must have been when bandsmen were being called upon to save democracy."

When Tex Beneke re-assembled the Miller Orchestra after the war, Mancini joined the famous ensemble. A few years later at Universal Studios he won his first Oscar nomination for his score for the *Glenn Miller Story* starring James Stewart.

In a dazzling ten-year period beginning in 1958 he had a succession of movie and TV hits. It began with his TV theme for *Peter Gunn* and his unusual blend of jazz and mood music. "It caught the public's ear," he explained. "They weren't used to hearing background music that was so distinctive." The theme for *Mr. Lucky* followed and was a similar TV hit. "I tell you when you're hot you're hot. It was incredible luck going from those scores to film assignments almost immediately, for *Breakfast at Tiffanys, Days of Wine and Roses, Hatarii* and *Pink Panther*—it was an incredible roll of luck."

When he wrote his most illustrious movie melody, "Moon River," the studio asked him whom he would like for a lyrical collaborator. "I went for the best and asked for Johnny Mercer. He not only had a firm grasp of the English language but also its colloquialisms. His lyrics were like poems. We worked together again on *Days of Wine and Roses* and won our second Oscar."

Mercer, like most lyricists, would listen to a melody before he put his words to paper. "It seems to throw them into rhyming schemes that follow the structure of the melody," Mancini explained. "I don't think Johnny would have thought of a line like 'my huckleberry friend,' if there hadn't been a turn in the melody at that point. Who knows where that came from? I'm sure it came to him because of the way the melody went at that point. The only score we did together that was a big disappointment to both of us was the Julie Andrews film *Darling Lili*. It was not a box-office hit for some inexplicable reason and consequently the music from the soundtrack never caught on."

As a pragmatist Mancini never considered his musical arrangements as timeless. "You put things down on record and it's there. But I'm sure long after I'm gone some young kid is going to listen to my tapes and say, 'wouldn't it be a great idea if we did this or that with those songs.' And I'm sure that's what's going to happen to the works of anyone who has recorded extensively."

During our last interview he reflected on his need to work and his lifelong love of writing and arranging. "My attitude is that we must keep trying as long as we can function. As far as I'm concerned the best is yet to come." It was a philosophy that left us a legacy of enduring Mancini melodies and timeless performances.

✪ ✪ ✪

Promoting the "Pink Panther Dolls" with Hank Mancini, 1981.

Meeting the legendary Orson Welles, Las Vegas, February 1980. (Photo by Rich Little)

"Your Obedient Servant," Orson Welles

Every October, as Halloween approaches, we are reminded that it was radio's most significant dramatic broadcast that made a household name of the incomparable Orson Welles. The night he terrified North America with his presentation of H.G. Wells' *The War of the Worlds* remains to this day a classic example of "theater of the mind."

With John Houseman, Welles founded the renowned Mercury Theater, and was on network radio with his own program when he was only 23. He was acclaimed by the critics as a "boy genius." His company of players included Agnes Moorehead, Vincent Price, Joseph Cotten, Everett Sloane and Ray Collins. They broadcast the classics in a way that they had never been presented before. His dramatizations revolutionized radio. The Mercury Theater repertory company, formed originally for the New York stage, followed him to Hollywood, where he astounded film makers with his dramatic new approach to movies as an art form.

In 1967 I had the opportunity to meet one of the members of the cast of *The War of the Worlds*, the late distinguished actress Agnes Moorehead (known to the TV generation as Endora of *Bewitched*), and reminisced back to her years with the Mercury Theater: "Because of *War of the Worlds* Orson was given carte blanche in Hollywood, and decided to go with RKO," she told me. "They offered him a picture on his own terms. He asked for certain stars to be in it, but because he was so young and if he was successful the stars felt they would not benefit from the film, and if he wasn't successful it would hurt their careers, so they turned him down. He responded by saying, 'well if that's the way you feel about it I'll get my own actors from New York.' So he called a number of us to go out to Hollywood. Of course, we had never been before a camera, but neither had he, for that matter."

On October 30, 1938, at 8:00 p.m. Eastern Standard Time, if audience ratings had remained normal, the majority of radio listeners would have tuned in to the *Chase & Sandborn Show* with Edgar Bergen and Charlie McCarthy. However, it was a terrifying abnormal evening for those brave souls who were listening at the same time to *The War of the Worlds*. The famous ventriloquist and radio comedian, Edgar Bergen, shortly before his death told me: "The *New York Times* wrote the following day 'anyone stupid enough not to be listening to Charlie McCarthy would be stupid enough to believe that the Martians were invading North America.' Years later I attended the Film Institute's salute to Orson and Charlie was still mad at him for stealing his audience."

Born in Kenosha, Wisconsin, May 6, 1915, Welles achieved genius status while still a young man. He appeared at the world-renowned Gate Theatre in Dublin when he was only 16, and on an American stage with Katherine Cornell before he had turned 20. He was 26 years old when he wrote, directed, produced and starred in his first film, *Citizen Kane*, considered by cinema buffs and historians as one of the best motion pictures ever made.

As a screen actor, Orson Welles will never be forgotten for his variety of roles in his own films and those of other film makers, like his Cardinal Wolsley in *A Man for All Seasons*, the lawyer in *Compulsion*, one of the Borgias in *Prince of Foxes*, and his small but dramatically charged part in *The Third Man* as the mysterious Harry Lime.

Years ago I attended a Dean Martin roast in Las Vegas, and flew back to Los Angeles with Rich Little on a plane that had an impressive passenger list, including Orson Welles, Gloria and Jimmy Stewart, Eddie Albert and Red Buttons. When we landed and disembarked, Welles had to wait for a baggage vehicle to take him from the plane to the entrance of the terminal—he couldn't walk that far and was too big for a wheelchair. As we were driving from the airport I saw him outside the building sitting on the vehicle, waiting for his limousine. He looked very lonely—almost abandoned.

After that meeting in Las Vegas, arrangements were made for me to interview him back in Los Angeles. However, a sudden storm swept in from the Pacific which brought down power lines, closed canyon roads and disrupted travel and communications. A few days later, he called me to make further arrangements, and in commenting on the devastation of the storm, actually said, in his most sonorous tones, "It was an act of God." It was such a dramatic statement I almost expected him to follow it with his famous sign-off "your obedient servant"—and then perhaps the heavens to open. To this day I deeply regret that I wasn't able to record our telephone conversation.

Married three times, he had a son, Christopher, to his first wife, and a daughter, Rebecca, to his second wife, Rita Hayworth. While he made a major contribution to motion pictures as an art form, pushing the limits of film making, he insisted that he preferred the theater to the screen.

A larger-than-life character, he accomplished a tour de force of cinematic style, storytelling and drama in *Citizen Kane*. He will always be remembered as the newspaper tycoon and political candidate who vowed to protect the underprivileged, underpaid and underfed.

To paraphrase a line from *Citizen Kane*, "as it must to all men, death came to" Orson Welles, October 10, 1985.

April 3, 1957—"The Day Elvis Came to Town."

The Day Elvis Came to Town

Every era has its entertainment "super stars," whose names are permanently linked to a period in time. For over two decades Elvis Presley was a phenomenal personality, who revolutionized popular music and left an indelible mark on the annals of show business. So great was his popularity that in a very real sense his spirit lingers on.

Since his death in 1977 he has been the subject of a vast collection of controversial books, articles and write-ups about his life and times. He has been dissected by the media to such an extent that it is difficult to separate fact from fiction. However, I do know that the polite young man I met and interviewed in 1957 was friendly, unpretentious and quite charming in a simple down-to-earth way.

That was the year of his Canadian tour and his reaction to the adulation of his fans revealed his warm personality and modest demeanor.

Well-mannered, he called me "sir" throughout our conversation, although I was only eight years his senior.

"Yes, this is my very first trip to Canada," he replied to my initial question. "I was in Toronto last night, and well, gee whiz, I was very much surprised at how wonderful the people are in this part of the country. I've been wanting to come up here; in fact, when they started bookin' the tour, I said by all means I want to go to Canada. About a year ago I tried to get them to book a tour up here, but I wasn't well known enough, so they figured I wouldn't make enough money if I came up here."

At the time of our interview I had been hosting a weekly radio program for "teens and twenties" called *The Campus Corner.* The promoters of the Presley tour asked me to introduce Elvis on stage. The show took place at what was Ottawa's hockey arena, The Auditorium, at Catherine and O'Connor Streets. It was demolished several years later to make way for the national headquarters of the YM-YWCA. Prior to the performance we met in a hockey locker room that had been converted into a makeshift dressing room. As I arrived Elvis was sitting on an old bench eating a plain cheese sandwich and holding a milk carton. With hordes of fans surrounding the building he couldn't get out for dinner. He was a prisoner of his own fame and remained so for the rest of his life.

About a year before the Presley company arrived, I had become a friend and enthusiastic supporter of a Lisgar Collegiate student, Rich Little, who was amazing everyone with his brilliant impressions. I am greatly indebted to him for preserving my Presley interview, since the original tape had been lost or erased in error in our radio archives.

Rich had recorded the interview on his own inexpensive tape machine while listening to my program. Twenty years later he was going through old files at his Malibu, California home and came across a tape with no markings on it. To his total surprise and mine it was his off-air copy of the Elvis interview—the same tape that he had played over and over again to perfect his impersonation of Presley's voice. I immediately had it brought up to broadcast quality, and just four months later at the time of Presley's sudden death, it was featured on radio stations across North America. Incidentally, I often hear portions of that interview without playing the tape, as Rich reconstucts our conversation doing both of our voices!

No one was more surprised at the Presley phenomenon than Elvis himself. I was curious whether he had given any thought to what it was that had made him an overnight success. "I sure have," he said without hesitation, "and in fact I don't even like to try and figure it out. I'm afraid if I find out what it is I might lose it, so I just keep guessing myself."

Being an only child, it had been reported that he was building a home for himself and his parents. "Well, I didn't build it," he told me, "I just bought it. It's an estate about ten miles from where I live now. Of course we had to have a larger place because I've accumulated so much junk in the last two years I had no place to put it." As everyone knows, his estate, which became Graceland, is now one of the most popular tourist attractions in the United States.

A personal exchange followed, which in retrospect is of interest, considering how his life unfolded. He was 22 at the time and one of the entertainment world's most eligible bachelors:

Gord: Do you have a girlfriend, may I ask?

Elvis: I don't have a special girlfriend. When I'm home I date a few different girls in Memphis, but I don't have a particular "one."

Gord: Have you given thought to the fact that some day you might meet a certain someone and decide that you would like to get married?

Elvis: I probably will.

Gord: Do you think it would hurt your popularity?

Elvis: (with a slight pause and laugh) It probably will.

Upon his arrival in Canada his latest recording, "All Shook Up," was shaking up the juke boxes. He was pleased to bring us up to date on its success: "It's sold a little over a million—it's about a million, two hundred thousand." His hit releases were appearing on both the pop and the country charts and I suggested his style was a blend of both. "Yes," he agreed. "It's an accumulation of both which has developed rock 'n' roll" (plus the influence of rhythm and blues). "It's rock 'n' roll which actually put me over." His reply to my comment was interesting since it was a comparatively new style of music at that time.

Listeners to *The Campus Corner* voted each week on the show for their favorite performers. Elvis was the undisputed winner for over a year. At the conclusion of our interview I presented him with a scroll proclaiming him the King of our Platter Poll and invited him to express his gratitude to those fans. "Well, I would like to tell them how deeply I appreciate their support. I've gotten more mail from Toronto, Ottawa and Montreal than any other area. I don't tell you that because I'm here; I have received more mail from Canada than I could ever count."

That evening the old hockey arena was jam-packed and shook to its shaky foundations with the screams and shouts of thousands of Presley followers. I will never appear on a stage to a more appreciative audience than that gathering on April 3, 1957. Words were quite unnecessary. I stepped on stage, opened my mouth to introduce him—but no one heard a word I said. They realized my appearance meant that Elvis was about to make his entrance and a cheer that erupted into an incredible roar almost put the building into orbit.

When the performance ended his handlers went into action with military precision—Elvis ran backstage where a station wagon with its tailgate down was waiting. The motor was running as he threw his guitar to a man crouched in the back of the vehicle and then he jumped into the station wagon and off they went. He was back in his suite at the Beacon Arms Hotel before any of his fans knew he had left the building. Hasty exits were his normal procedure for the next 20 years of his often turbulent life.

He was born January 8, 1935, in Tupelo, Mississippi, and christened Elvis Aaron. His father, Vernon, worked at a variety of jobs during the Depression. His mother, Gladys, doted on her only child (a twin boy was stillborn) and he in turn was a devoted son. Conditions were so poor in their rural area, with almost everyone on relief, that they moved to Memphis in hopes of a better life. It was there that young Elvis was greatly influenced by both gospel and country music. A birthday gift of a second-hand guitar from his parents intensified his interest in music.

While working as a truck driver in 1953, he paid four dollars to a local studio to record two songs as a surprise gift for his mother. A short time later he was signed to a contract by Sam Phillips of Sun Records, who once said that Presley combined "innocence and impudence in those early years." Under the guidance of his astute manager, "Colonel" Tom Parker, his recording contract was purchased by RCA Victor, who launched his international career. Television appearances on shows hosted by Tommy and Jimmy Dorsey and Ed Sullivan made him an overnight sensation.

In those formative years Pat Boone was Presley's biggest competitor. Their public personas were the opposite sides of a juke-box coin, from white bucks to blue suede shoes. But they were only rivals in the minds of their respective fans.

"Elvis and I had known each other before his widely known public career started," Boone told me in an interview following Presley's death. "He had a sort of country-western following before he made *Heartbreak Hotel*, so I knew him back in the very early days and our friendship continued right along. We sometimes rented or leased houses less than a mile apart in Bel Air, a rather exclusive area of Los Angeles. He would come over on a summer afternoon just to sit around and see me and my wife Shirley and the kids playing. He wasn't married yet and was getting close to thirty and I think he really envied our family life. Of course, he eventually married [Priscilla] and he had a daughter [Lisa Marie]. We didn't visit too much during the last two or three years of his life."

Across the Atlantic an aspiring young singer fell under the spell of the King of Rock 'n' Roll. Years later in Las Vegas they became friends—by that time Jerry Dorsey was known as England's Englebert Humperdinck. "Whenever Elvis was in town I would go to see him and he would come to my show. Of all the entertainers I have seen on stage, and I do apologize if I am hurting anyone by saying this, he was the most exciting entertainer I've ever met, and one of the most affectionate in private life."

Rich Little also attended Presley performances and visited him backstage. "I've always thought Elvis was a real charmer. I met him twice. The last time was about a year before he died. He was at the Hilton and I talked with him about a number of things for about an hour. The first time I was introduced to him he said to his staff, 'Gee, I don't want to talk to him, it's like talking to myself,' then he winked at me and everybody laughed.

"As you can tell, Gord, from the interview you did with him, he was very polite and most hospitable. There was nothing phony about him and he was friendly with everyone. But I must say that while he had everything—fame, fortune and the love of people all over the world—it seems most of the time he was a very lonely man, who rarely went anywhere and lived in seclusion. In that respect I felt sorry for him."

The last time Pat Boone saw his old friendly rival he was shocked at his appearance and physical deterioration. "It was just a few months before he died and we met in Memphis airport. He looked real bad. He was on his way to Las Vegas and Shirley, the girls and I were going to Florida. We laughed and kidded a bit and I slapped him on the stomach and asked him, 'What's this all about?' I didn't know how serious his condition was, and he said, 'Ah, I've been eating too well, I'll sweat it out in Vegas. Where are you going?' I told him Orlando, and he said, 'Man, that's the wrong way! But you were always going the wrong way, weren't you?' Everybody laughed and I said, 'Well, Elvis, it all depends on where you are coming from.' We laughed, because we realized we were making some wry comments about the way the public saw us, but we also knew that we shared the same philosophy, and the same belief in God and the important and meaningful things in life."

Elvis Presley was just 42 years old when he died at his Graceland mansion, August 16, 1977.

"The way we were"—a reunion with The Four Aces, March 1979.

"FOREVER" THE FOUR ACES

The nostalgic hit musical *Forever Plaid* is a unique theatrical experience that is both a spoof and a tribute to a bygone era of show business. Audiences across North America have been captivated by the show's talented quartet of performers who rekindle the songs and the vocal groups of the 1950s and 1960s. Of all the recording artists they revive with close harmony, exaggerated vocal tricks and choreography, none is more fondly recalled than The Four Aces.

Back in those happy days when rock was a new musical fad and the hit parade belonged to Tin Pan Alley, four personable young men from the Philadelphia area were the most popular vocal group in the world. We became close friends and have remained so down through the years.

The Four Aces were favorites with audiences of all ages. The bass in the quartet, Lou Silvestri, remembers those engagements vividly. "When we were working at the top clubs across the continent, we always seemed to have a new hit record that everyone wanted to hear. The fans were very supportive. We enjoyed similar success in Europe and especially in Britain."

Al Alberts, the lead vocalist with The Aces, was a band singer early in his career. During World War II, while serving in the U.S. Coast Guard in Newfoundland, he met Dave Mahoney, who was from his home town, Chester, Pennsylvania. After their discharge they decided to form a musical combo. They convinced two friends, Sod Vaccaro and Lou Silvestri, to join them in their showbiz endeavor. Oddly enough the foursome began as an instrumental group. "Well, Lou was our drummer," Al recalled, "Sod our trumpet player and I was the piano player and occasional vocalist. Dave, who was our saxophonist, was once voted by *Downbeat* magazine as one of the best jazz musicians in the business."

Al has always been amazed at how easily they switched from their roles as musicians to a close-knit vocal ensemble. "The Aces came about as if by fate. It's quite possible that among four musicians one of them, or all of them, can't sing. It's also likely that three of them might be baritones or all of them might be tenors. It is also difficult to locate a top tenor voice, which is quite unique. Well, when we first attempted to sing as a quartet we were very surprised to discover that we had a bass, a baritone, a top tenor and a lead voice. When we recorded our first hit record, 'It's No Sin,' we had a natural blend of voices. It was an amazing discovery."

As Dave recalls, their first record came about through unusual circumstances. "We were playing in a club in a coal mining area of Pennsylvania where polka music was very popular. The manager insisted that every night we had to play at least one polka. A friend of ours who was a local musician and songwriter, George Hogan, offered to arrange a few polkas for us provided we featured one of his songs in our act. We did, and 'It's No Sin' won us a Decca recording contract."

The Aces had the golden touch, with five of their releases selling over one million copies. "It's No Sin" was followed by "Tell Me Why," "Stranger in Paradise," "Three Coins in the Fountain" and their biggest hit, "Love Is a Many Splendored Thing." They were so popular that they appeared 12 times on the Ed Sullivan Show and were Jackie Gleason's guests 10 times.

The familiar shuffle beat identified most of their arrangements and their performances were always well choreographed. "Al was associated early in his career as a vocalist with the Jan Savitt Orchestra," Sod reminded me. "It was a band that popularized shuffle, and when we began writing our arrangements, although we never planned on making it our beat—it just happened."

During one of my many interviews with The Aces I recalled that they were the first group to concentrate on choreography. "Gord," Al said with a laugh, "we have been criticized for that. The reason why we developed choreography is quite amusing. Visualize a piano player who had never left the keyboard, a drummer who always had sticks in his hands and a trumpet player and saxophonist who always had their instruments in hand, then have them set aside their musical props, as we did, and you can imagine how uncomfortable we felt not knowing what to do with our hands. We were awkward performing, so we decided to hire a choreographer to make sure we were all doing the same thing at the same time. We never dreamed then that we would end up doing dance steps. But that's how it started, because we didn't know what to do with our hands."

During two nostalgia tours in 1978 and 1980, The Four Aces were enthusiastically received with "sold-out" houses wherever they appeared.

With the exception of Al, who hosts a very popular TV talent show in Philadelphia, the fellows have left the entertainment business for various business ventures and semi-retirement. But along with their wives and families they often recall fondly those golden years of The Four Aces. Their beautiful melodies linger on like old friends from happy days gone by.

Rosemary Clooney with two of her biggest fans, Elaine and Gord Atkinson, 1984.

An Incomparable Lady of Song

During the 1950s Rosemary Clooney was a Paramount film star, radio and television headliner and a consistent hit maker. Forty years later she is being universally acclaimed by musicologists and fans alike as one of the great popular singers of the 20th century. Over the years she has also gained respect and admiration in the critical world of jazz. Frank Sinatra once said, "Rosemary has that great talent which exudes warmth and feeling in every song she sings. She's a symbol of good modern music." Bing Crosby, shortly before his death, praised her as "the best singer in the business!"

In 1995 she received excellent reviews for her sensitive acting skills on the TV medical drama *ER* portraying a once-famous singer suffering from Alzheimer's disease. Oscar-winning director Steven Spielberg was so impressed with her characterization that he sent her a fan letter. Her guest role was suggested by her nephew, George Clooney, her brother's son, who portrays Dr. Doug Ross on the ongoing hit series.

In December 1995 she concluded a successful year-long national U.S. tour, which celebrated the 40th anniversary of the making of the yuletide movie musical *White Christmas* at New York's Lincoln Center. The large company that she assembled for the tour included her daughter-in-law, Debby Boone, four of her eight grandchildren, two choral groups and a full orchestra.

Every Christmas for several years now she has recorded an appropriate ballad for distribution to her friends as a thoughtful remembrance. Each cassette has a personal greeting and they have become rare collector's items.

Rosemary began her professional singing career with her late sister Betty during the final days of the big band era. They were a popular singing duo with Tony Pastor's Orchestra.

Married to the late internationally acclaimed actor Jose Ferrer, and the mother of five young children, her personal life was shattered with the breakup of their marriage. The extraordinary demands of her career caused further stress to her state of mind, which resulted in a terrifying mental breakdown. Her account of that period of despair was revealed candidly in her autobiography. With self-determination, proper medical treatment, and the help of concerned and understanding relatives and friends, she made a complete recovery—followed by an inspiring show business comeback.

Her fascinating story, *This for Remembrance*, which was adapted as a TV movie, took its title from a line from Shakespeare's *Hamlet*. It's a story that has helped people to overcome adversity and conquer an illness that can strike anyone. She never hesitates to offer encouragement to those in need.

In one of our interviews she remembeed fondly the support she received from her colleagues—two in particular: "When I was hospitalized they somehow found out where I was—one was Bob Hope, who sent me a huge bouquet of flowers with a note that said, 'I hope it's a boy!' About a week later a letter came from Bing Crosby, who was in England and heard about my illness. In his words of encouragement he said, 'If there is anything you need I'm here for you!'—And that's the way he was.

"It's such a relief when you finally accept your medical condition and realize that you are not the only one who has ever felt or thought the way you do. That's the point that pleased me the most about writing the book. So many people came up to me and said, 'I really didn't know that anyone else felt these things until I read your book.' The television drama elicited a similar reaction."

In 1980 Rosemary and her journalist brother Nick (who is a TV host on the American Movie Classics Channel) launched an annual star-studded fund-raiser on behalf of The Betty Clooney Foundation for the Brain Injured—The Singers' Salute to the Songwriters. Their sister Betty died as a result of a brain aneurysm in 1976.

In the 1950s, under the tutelage of Mitch Miller, who was the artists and repertoire director of Columbia Records, a number of Clooney hits were produced. They ran the musical gamut from "Come-on-a My House" to her beautifully performed ballads, "Hey There," "Mixed Emotions" and "Tenderly."

"I love 'Tenderly,' but it's a difficult song to sing and I wasn't relaxed with it. Mitch was a great director. He would never just flip on the 'talkback' and speak to you through the studio window. He would come out of the booth and talk to you quietly, which is a sign of a good director. He told me that I was letting the song intimidate me. 'You are not singing it,' he said, 'It's singing you.' Mine was the 29th record of 'Tenderly' and he said, 'You have just got to pretend that Walter Gross and Jack Lawrence wrote it for you and it has never been recorded before.' And that was the way I approached it and we got it on the next take. But Mitch really knew what to say to me."

My association with Rosemary dates back to the 1970s when I was producing *The Crosby Years*. Bing played a major role in her early career on radio and TV and co-starred with her and Danny Kaye in *White Christmas*. It was during his 50th anniversary tours of North America and Britain in 1976-77 that Rosemary resumed her career. Bing was largely responsible for her return to show business. He also wrote the foreword to her autobiography. With his encouragement and the support of producers and musician friends, she has recorded an impressive collection of albums over the years for the Concord jazz label.

"We were all in awe of Bing," Rosemary recalled. "By the time I arrived in Hollywood, he was a legendary figure yet he never was comfortable with that image. Danny was an enormously talented man, but Danny felt the same way about Bing as I did. I remember once talking to Frank Sinatra about Bing and he said, 'How can you be so comfortable with him; you seem quite at ease in his company.' And I assured him that I was just pretending to be relaxed. Bing, of course, was the person who least wanted that kind of adulation. He really was a modest man. It's hard to say that about a star of his magnitude but it is true. He was wonderful with fans. When I appeared with him at the London Palladium he would meet them at the stage door and sign autographs late into the evening."

The last line of the Clooney biography refers to "This Ol' House," which of course was the title of one of her big novelty numbers, but it is also a fond reference to her home. The house where she raised her five children has a fascinating history. Built by one of the pioneers of Beverly Hills, Monte Blue, it was once the residence of George Gershwin, who, with his brother Ira, wrote two everlasting ballads in the living room, "A Foggy Day" and "Love Is Here to Stay." Ira eventually bought the house next door and was Rosemary's neighbor until his death.

"One day when Ira was visiting us we were sitting in the living room and he told us that our piano was in the same place where George had placed his piano. The last song they wrote together was 'Our Love Is Here to Stay.' The house was the first one built in Beverly Hills. Russ Columbo, one of the early crooners, was killed in the den. He was visiting a writer friend who lived in our house at that time and while examining a Civil War rifle was shot in a freak accident. Apparently the gun was rusted shut, but by some odd set of circumstances it discharged and the charge ricocheted off the wall and killed him. It was a tragedy that rocked Hollywood." (The house, incidentally, was the subject of one of Edward R. Murrow's famous *Person to Person* TV broadcasts.)

Nat Cole was a frequent guest of Rosemary and Jose Ferrer and after every dinner party played Gershwin melodies on their piano. "He was so wonderful. His wife Maria was a lovely lady. Every Monday night we would have about eight people for dinner. Nat never had coffee or dessert, so while we were still at the table he would go into the living room and play the piano for our pleasure. I must say it was an overabundance of good fortune to be serenaded that way—what serendipity!"

Rosemary is a very proud mother and grandmother. The marriage of Shirley and Pat Boone's daughter Debby to her son Gabriel Ferrer united two popular show business families.

At a time of life when most singers have difficulty living up to their past reputations, Rosemary has never sounded better. Critics are unanimous that she is singing today with more feeling and assurance than at any time in her career.

During one of our conversations she reflected on her current acclaim: "I think, somehow, having a longer view and more experience helps, and the fact that there is a kind of joy to my work now. It was missing in the past, diverted at times with the attention I had to give to my children, and other stressful things that were going on in my life. Now I feel that music is the most important thing in my life, and it gives me great joy."

"A Shining Talent"—Tony Bennett following a 1986 concert.

A Singer's Singer

Frank Sinatra once called Tony Bennett "the best singer in the business, the best exponent of song." Later he capped that glowing comment with more revealing words about his admiration for Bennett's artistry: "He excites me whenever I watch him—he moves me." Years ago Bing Crosby told me, during one of our interviews, that Bennett was one of his all-time favorite performers and "a shining talent!"

He has long been considered a "singer's singer," and is one of the most popular and respected figures in the world of music. Anyone who has attended one of his concerts has fallen under the spell of the Bennett magic. He illuminates theaters and nightclubs with his supercharged energy. His phrasing is exquisite, his diction and enunciation beyond reproach. His choice of material has always reflected his flawless taste.

I once asked him what ingredients he looked for in choosing a song: "It's the craftsmanship, the cleverness, how well it's written, how vital the song feels," he replied. "I look for incongruous melodies. Advertisers often say 'make it simple and not complicated,' and yet the most popular and one of the most beautiful ballads ever written, 'Stardust,' is a complicated melody in its structure."

Throughout our parallel careers we have met several times, socially and for radio interviews, beginning back in the 1950s.

A native of Astoria, New York, one of his more recent record albums took him back to his old neighborhood for a sentimental collection of the songs of his youth. He was born Anthony Dominick Benedetto, August 3, 1926. His father, a tailor from Calabria, emigrated to New York City, where in time he changed occupations and opened a grocery store. He recognized early that Tony had an excellent natural singing voice and encouraged him to pursue music. His older son, John, had formal voice training.

While attending high school, where he studied industrial art in hopes of becoming a commercial artist, Tony supplemented his family's income with weekend singing engagements. His Dad died at a relatively young age, and his mother, out of necessity, worked as a seamstress, while his sister Mary looked after the household chores.

Shortly after he graduated Tony was inducted into the army, and spent the last three months of World War II in Europe. As an infantryman he witnessed the devastation of Europe, which molded his social conscience. He is well known for his fund-raising concerts on behalf of worthy causes around the world.

One of the famous winners on Arthur Godfrey's well-remembered *Talent Scouts* program, Tony, in a competition among all winners for one year, placed second to Rosemary Clooney. Recalling the song he featured that night, the old standard "I May Be Wrong," he said with good humor, "The title couldn't have been more appropriate, I sure was wrong—Rosie was great and she won!" A few years later they co-starred on a nightly 15-minute radio show.

It was a series of appearances at Greenwich Village clubs that proved to be the turning point in his career. Critical acclaim brought him to the attention first of Pearl Bailey, and then Bob Hope, who invited him to join his cast for an engagement at Manhattan's Paramount Theater. A Columbia recording contract followed a short time later.

The first Bennett hit ballad was the torchy lament "The Boulevard of Broken Dreams," followed by "Cold, Cold Heart," "Because of You," and "Rags to Riches." An impressive number of exceptional ballads have become all-time favorites, thanks to Tony. His personal musical crusade has been to keep alive the songs of the great classic popular composers, while at the same time introducing ballads by promising new composers.

In 1963 he achieved both aims with one song, a collaboration between the great lyracist Johnny Mercer and an amateur writer: "A charming lady from Youngstown, Ohio, Sadie Vimmerstedt was a big fan of Johnny Mercer and she came up with a line that she thought sounded like a Mercer title, 'I Wanna Be Around to Pick up the Pieces, When Somebody Breaks Your Heart.' So she wrote a fan letter to him and asked him to consider the line for one of his songs. Johnny was knocked out with the phrase, wrote the song with her and gave her 50 per cent of the profits. It was my follow-up hit to 'San Francisco,' so Sadie made a gang of money. She loved to travel, and enjoyed several wonderful trips from her royalties. She sent me cards from all over the world. Whenever I return to Youngstown to perform, as I'm singing, through the spotlight I'll see someone waving, and I know it's Sadie!"

Tony has also been widely recognized as an artist with brush and pallet. His landscape paintings have sold for considerable sums of money, and his works have been displayed in prominent galleries.

The ballad that became his biggest hit and his signature song was released at the height of Beatlemania. "It was 1963," Tony reminisced, "and the hit parade was dominated by rock 'n' roll, and this beautiful melody became the hit of the year. It just proved to me that you must believe in yourself. Despite obstacles and trends, you must have confidence in what you are doing."

At first Tony admits he didn't recognize the potential of his most requested song, "I Left My Heart in San Francisco." "My music director, Ralph Sharon, who has found almost all my songs over the years, brought this beautiful anthem to 'The City by the Bay' to my attention. We were going to San Francisco," Tony remembered, "and I thought it would be a great song to feature at the Fairmont Hotel, thinking of it, however, as only a local song. We actually auditioned it while we were completing an engagement in Hot Springs, Arkansas. One of the bartenders at our hotel overheard our rehearsal and said to me, 'Tony, if you record that song I'll go out and buy a copy.' Actually I thought the other side of the eventual record would be the hit, the lovely ballad 'Once Upon a Time.' It only proves," Tony added with a smile, "that you should always listen to the advice of your friendly bartender—they know what's happening."

In the years before electronics enhanced the art of vocalizing, a singer's performance was judged, by patrons and critics alike, by the performer's ability to fill a theater with his or her voice. Tony tells a wonderful anecdote about emulating his legendary predecessors.

"Another group, whose advice I take seriously, are the taxi cab drivers in New York City. People are often annoyed with the way they talk while conducting business, but to me they are great natural philosophers. For example, something I do on stage that seems to impress everyone enormously is sing a couple of songs without a microphone. I was encouraged to do that during my concerts by a cabby who said to me, 'Tony, these new singers are bums—they can't perform without a microphone and amplification. They need electronic gimmicks to make them sound okay. The real oldtimers, like Al Jolson and Ethel Merman, used to hit the back of the house with sheer lung power; they didn't need a microphone.' It was from that comment, during a trip across Manhattan, that I decided to sing on stage without a microphone as a tribute to the stars of the past."

Red Buttons and Tony Bennett join me for lunch and conversation at the Las Vegas Hilton Hotel, March 1974.

Rich Little "on air" imitating program host Gord Atkinson. (Were we having a problem hearing?)

Canada's Ambassador of Good Humor

One of my closest friends is a friend of legendary stars and prominent politicians. He is indeed the alter ego of the famous personalities of our time. He is also the entertainment world's most popular impressionist-comedian, and Canada's unofficial ambassador of good humor.

Rich Little is also a frequent supporter of worthy causes, especially in his home-town Ottawa. He returns to the capital whenever his busy schedule permits. Wherever his international travels take him he proudly proclaims his Canadian identity.

He has raised the gift of mimicry to an art form. His impressions are so accurate and so amazing that he has recorded movie soundtrack dialogue for ailing stars like David Niven and Peter Sellers without the public realizing they were listening to his voice.

Because of our mutual interest in the entertainment business and his friendship with the stars, he often puts me in contact with them—and on occasion has joined me during my interview sessions. I refer to him (only half in jest) as my Hollywood agent.

We have a great deal in common, including a tendency to be forgetful. At times we have difficulty remembering where we placed essential items like our wallets and car keys. Travel directions are seldom remembered by either one of us and we have lost our way all over North America. I'm guilty of not always paying attention to directions, but Rich has trouble following a map. Sometimes I believe he thinks that "Rand-McNally" was an old vaudeville act!

I first met Rich when he was attending the capital's oldest high school, Lisgar Collegiate, and I was hosting an Ottawa radio show for teenagers. With fellow impersonator and boyhood buddy Geoff Scott, he made his showbiz debut on that program in the fall of 1956.

The youthful team of Little & Scott surprised and amazed both teens and their parents with a repertoire of famous voices that included political leaders, movie stars and TV's reigning emcee, Ed Sullivan. Each week on the radio show they presented adaptations of current movies—doing the voices of the stars and the sound effects! "We really honed our raw talent on those programs," Rich recalls. "Radio gave us an opportunity to develop what is not available today to most young performers. It was really theater of the mind back then." Following their eventual national acclaim on television, Rich hit the road to Hollywood, while Geoff pursued a career as a journalist.

Over the years I have received amusing phone calls and listened to the simulated voices of stars and politicians on the other end of the line. These conversations with Rich happened often when I was a gullible young writer-broadcaster and he was a high school prankster. Often I would be greeted on the phone by John Wayne, then suddenly be talking to Humphrey Bogart, George Burns or James Mason. On a few occasions I have received a call from a celebrity, and wondered throughout the conversation if I was really talking to a well-known personality or if it was just another fun call from Rich.

In the 1970s when I was producing the Crosby radio anthology, I took a call from California and talked to Bing for several minutes before I was convinced that I wasn't talking to Rich. Bing thought my predicament was very funny.

Rich's incredible collection of over 300 voices includes a devastating impression of yours truly, so I've often heard a conversation on the phone between Bing and me—without opening my mouth! My interview with Elvis Presley is often reconstructed by him so that I may experience another telephone session of déjà vu.

When a Little impression is being developed he will work on the subject with the aid of a tape recorder to perfect his impersonation. "Sometimes it can take me months to develop a difficult voice," Rich admits, "while other times I'll duplicate a more obvious voice in a matter of minutes. The singing voices are my greatest challenge. It's strange, but when I sing like Robert Goulet, for example, I can hit notes that are beyond my normal range. I always try to capture the personality and mannerisms of a celebrity from 'the inside out' rather than do just a caricature of that person."

Although the Little family had no theatrical background, Rich had a solid and thorough training as an actor during his formative years. He has high praise for the guidance and experience he gained at The Ottawa Little Theatre, where he appeared in both dramatic and comedic roles. "Everything I know about acting was developed from those early years," he says with affection when discussing his apprenticeship with the local theatrical institution. "I was fortunate to learn my trade from a very professional group of directors and actors." Incidentally, there is no connection between his name and the name of the venerable theater. But it is true that another young thespian once accused him of getting all the good parts because he mistakenly thought that his Dad owned The Ottawa Little Theatre.

When Rich was growing up the family residence was at a choice Ottawa location on the scenic driveway that parallels the historic Rideau Canal. His late father was a prominent doctor, navy veteran and accomplished athlete, who played football briefly for the Ottawa Roughriders. His mother has lived for many years in a lovely condominium apartment overlooking the St. Lawrence River in Brockville, Ontario, where many of her relatives and friends reside. Elizabeth Little, who is "Mama" to all who know and love her, celebrated her

93rd birthday May 18, 1996. She recalls with love and humor Rich's boyhood years:

"He was someone different every week—he would imitate for days the latest star he had seen at the Saturday matinée. I would have to drag him and his brothers out of our neighborhood theatre or they would sit through the same movie two or three times. The manager got to know us very well."

Rich's older brother Fred is also a popular impressionist well known to Canadian audiences; the younger Little brother, Chris, is involved in public relations and acting. Both brothers have appeared professionally with Rich.

When he was attending Lisgar Collegiate Rich began imitating his teachers, who were his first victims of impersonation. As he remembers, with tongue-in-cheek, "There was a concentrated campaign among faculty members to graduate me early." All was forgiven, however, when he returned to his alma mater for the school's 140th anniversary with an old friend and fellow Lisgarite, the late Lorne Greene. Another acclaimed classmate, Peter Jennings, was unable to attend the campus gathering because of his ABC-TV news commitments.

One summer during his teen years Rich worked as a movie usher at an Ottawa cinema landmark, the Elgin Theatre. He recorded the dialogue from the films on view and memorized favorite lines by his favorite stars. "My employment, however, was terminated abruptly," he recalls, "when one evening I accidentally rewound my tape recorder and its high speed whining sound was heard throughout a packed theater."

All that summer he perfected one of his most famous voices by asking his mother at every opportunity, in the familiar drawl of James Stewart, for "a piece of apple pie." Today, Rich counts the greatly respected star among his closest friends and most ardent supporters. A few years ago Rich arranged an interview for me with Mr. Stewart at his home in Beverly Hills. Following our visit, which included Rich delighting our host with lines from his films, we were leaving his house when a tour bus stopped in front. We could hear the driver pointing out the Stewart home to his passengers. Suddenly one of the tourists on board spotted Rich and called out to him, "Rich! What are you doing at Jimmy Stewart's house?" Without missing a beat, Rich replied, "Oh, I was just in there getting my batteries re-charged."

One of Rich's special interests through the years has been the work of the Boy Scouts of Canada. His Dad was very involved in the movement and the three Little brothers were all active scouts; Rich achieved the highest scout ranking. He is often a spokesman for the Boy Scouts in both Canada and the United States.

During his apprenticeship as an entertainer he was often on the same bill as another Ottawa native who became an international headliner, Paul Anka. Since they both made their radio debut on my old radio show we have had a few fun-filled reunions over the years in Ottawa and Las Vegas. Of course Rich would liven the occasion by doing a takeoff of me conversing with Paul!

The Little record library began over 30 years ago when he and fellow broadcaster, Les Lye, produced Canada's all-time best-selling political comedy album *My Fellow Canadians*—a salutation made famous by Prime Minister John Diefenbaker. His American LPs have been inspired by the administrations of Presidents Nixon, Ford, Carter, Reagan, Bush and Clinton, who are all featured in his nightclub act. A White House guest of the Reagans on four occasions, he was also among the guest performers at White House gatherings for Mr. and Mrs. Bush.

"With a few notable exceptions," Rich reveals, "the people I like to impersonate are the people I admire the most. Like a caricaturist I exaggerate the speech pattern and quality of a person's voice and magnify their mannerisms, but I never intentionally ridicule anyone. Audiences laugh along with me and the person being satirized. Many of the celebrities that I impersonate are among my biggest fans. I can only think of a couple of people who were less than enthusiastic about my impression of them—John Diefenbaker and Richard Nixon I was told were not amused at first, but they eventually came around when they realized I treated all politicians in the same irreverent manner."

Through the persistent efforts of one of his earliest supporters, Mel Tormé, Rich made his American TV debut on *The Judy Garland Show* in 1964. Tormé was the choral director and a frequent co-star on that program. The Little guest spot was so electrifying that overnight Rich became the most sought-after performer in Hollywood, sharing the spotlight on variety shows with his boyhood comedy idols Jack Benny, George Burns and Bob Hope.

By 1972 he was acclaimed as the "Comedy Star of the Year" by the American Guild of Variety Artists. Tormé recalls that the first time he heard Rich perform he was "stunned and amazed by his incredible talent for mimicry." He remembers with astonishment that "He not only did all the great stars, but duplicated the voices of the screen's little-known character actors. At my request he recorded all these voices for me, knowing that I shared his love of the movies and film makers. I treasure that tape to this day."

The recipient of entertainment and humanitarian awards, Rich gives freely of his time and talent for worthy causes, and has raised millions of dollars for charitable events. The profits from his unforgettable concert with Frank Sinatra in 1982 built the "Rich Little Special Care Nursery" at Ottawa's Civic Hospital. "That was one of the highwater marks of my life and career," he proudly states. Rich was born at the Civic, November 26, 1938, and shares the same birthday (but a different year) with one of his favorite "voices" and friends, Robert Goulet.

His benefit performances have also funded an ongoing medical program at Brockville's St. Vincent de Paul Hospital, and a scholarship bursary for young artists and performers at the Centrepointe Theatre in Nepean, Ontario.

Ottawa's perennial showbiz son has received the "key to the city," had a day proclaimed in his name during an official homecoming, and had a street named in his honor. In January 1992, he was honored at a testimonial dinner for disadvantaged children by the Variety Club of Ottawa. He has also been feted for charity by another theatrical institution, The Friars Club, in both New York and Los Angeles.

A resident of the California movie colony of Malibu for 20 years, where he had two residences, an impressive seaside home and a more spectacular cliff-side estate, a few years ago he moved to Las Vegas where he built a Spanish-style home in a secluded desert community. It was an appropriate change of address since he spends a great deal of his performing time in the casino capital.

Although he is divorced from his English-born wife, Jeanne, their relationship is cordial. They are the proud parents of a pretty, adult daughter, Bria, who visits her famous father at every opportunity. When she was a little girl he would read fairy tales and sing nursery rhymes for her in the voices of screen stars, politicians and cartoon characters. Richard Nixon reciting "Jack and Jill" was a particularly hilarious favorite and a stellar bedtime Little performance.

Despite changing attitudes and trends Rich feels confident that his unique brand of entertainment will pass the test of time, as he constantly adds new voices to his incredible repertoire, while preserving the famous voices of the past. In paraphrasing a familiar poetic line, Rich says, "Laugh along with me—the best is yet to come!"

Rich doesn't do impersonations in normal conversations today as he did years ago. However, now and then he will catch someone off guard and try to convince them that he is someone else. Early in our friendship this was a common occurrence.

One of my favorite memories happened on a Saturday morning when our children were young. After a sleepless night with our infant daughter, one of our boys woke me up to tell me someone was calling me on the phone. He looked rather confused and said with disbelief in his voice, "It's a funny call; the man sounds just like you!" He thought about this strange situation for a moment and then said matter-of-factly, "Oh, it's probably Uncle Rich." I asked him what he said to him, and my son, Paul, replied with laughter in his voice, "He told me to go into the bedroom and see if I'm up yet!" Well, ever since that confusing and amusing call so many years ago I have always "been up" for my buddy Rich.

✪ ✪ ✪

The Civic Hospital Gala—our patron/host Prime Minister Pierre Trudeau, Elaine and Gord Atkinson and Rich Little (Photo John Evans).

"The poet laureate of popular music"—my dear friend, Sammy Cahn.

A Poet Laureate of Tin Pan Alley

If the world of popular music should ever bestow the title of "Poet Laureate" on its legendary writers, that honor will be posthumously bestowed by acclamation on Sammy Cahn. An outstanding lyricist for the past six decades, he was one of the most prolific songwriters of the 20th century. His lyrics are as familiar to the public as many of the classical poems and sonnets of the English language. Within the industry that he loved he was always in demand, writing special material for those occasions when Tin Pan Alley would pay tribute to his fellow writers and performers.

The world of music skipped a beat January 15, 1993, when my friend of 20 years died of heart failure at a youthful 79 in Los Angeles.

Sammy Cahn

Our association began in 1972 when he accompanied Paul Anka back to his home town for an Ottawa engagement. He was Paul's songwriting mentor and occasional collaborator—they co-authored Frank Sinatra's comeback song, "Let Me Try Again." From our mutual acquaintance with the Anka family our friendship grew over the years, culminating in a series of lengthy interviews about his life and times.

In one of those conversations he paid tribute to his collaborators: "I have been working with gifted composers since the early 1930s and I have fixed and definite opinions about lyric writing. For instance, I believe that a word is only as good as the note it sits on, and all my life I have been blessed with the best notes. The words and music must be a perfect match. You read a poem, you must sing a lyric. For me the joy of singing a lyric is my greatest reward." The melodies that complement his words were penned by a disparate, highly talented group of partners, including Saul Chaplin ("Bei Mir Bist Du Schön"), Nicholas Brodsky ("Be My Love"), Jule Styne ("I've Heard That Song Before") and James Van Heusen ("My Kind of Town").

The only five-time winner of the Academy Award for the best song of the year, he shared that honor with Styne in 1954 for the title tune of "Three Coins in the Fountain," and with Van Heusen for "All the Way" (1957), "High Hopes" (1959) and "Call Me Irresponsible" (1963). He had a staggering 30 Oscar nominations. In addition to their movie Oscars, the team of Cahn and Van Heusen won the only Emmy award given by the TV academy for an original song, "Love and Marriage," from the 1955 production of *Our Town*.

In referring to Irving Berlin's incomparable body of work, Sammy once said to me with wonderment in his voice, "If a man in a lifetime of writing popular songs can point to six standard songs, he has done a remarkable job. Berlin wrote about 60 great standards!" That quote can be paraphrased as an appropriate Cahn epitaph, for his own lyrical output was truly amazing. Among his three dozen enduring ballads and novelties are lasting titles like "I'll Walk Alone," "Until the Real Thing Comes Along," "Saturday Night is the Loneliest Night of the Week," "It's Been a Long, Long Time," "Day By Day," "Time After Time," "It's Magic," "Five Minutes More," "Come Fly with Me," "The Second Time Around," "The Tender Trap," etc., etc.

His songs were often written with a particular person in mind and they were popularized by a "who's who" of show business, including Doris Day, Judy Garland, Bing Crosby, Mario Lanza, Julie Andrews, Dean Martin, Sammy Davis and, most of all, Frank Sinatra.

Sammy took no chances when trying to convince a performer to feature one of his songs. He would not depend on someone else to audition his material—he would sing the lyrics lustily in his pleasing but limited range to the amazement of those in attendance. "When Mario Lanza was the toast of MGM I went to his office and introduced him to the ballad that became his biggest hit. As I struggled on the high notes I could see his discomfort as he glared at me with those dark eyes in disbelief, while I continued to attack the melody. Later I laughed about my performance, but even my shaky rendition couldn't kill his intense interest in this dramatic ballad of operatic dimensions, 'Be My Love.'"

With fellow lyricist Johnny Mercer he founded the National Academy of Popular Music and the New York Song Writer's Hall of Fame, and was the driving force in organizing the Academy's annual dinner to induct writers and performers onto their honor roll of sharps and flats. For example, at the 1982 ceremonies that I attended, the honorees were Harold Arlen, Gordon Jenkins, Tony Bennett, Dinah Shore, Bob Dylan and Paul Simon.

Cahn ballads have a distinctive theatrical sound and dramatic endings. "Being around vaudeville in my youth I picked up the vaudeville traditions," Sammy revealed, "and my songs have vaudeville endings. For example, the last lines of "All the Way" and "Three Coins in the Fountain" build to a climax; I give the singer the get-off notes and an invitation from the audience for applause.

"When people ask me the inevitable question, 'which comes first, the words or the music,' I answer, and not as facetiously as it may sound, the phone call! With few exceptions every song that I have co-written has come about because of a phone call from a performer or studio requesting new material, or one of my collaborators calling while in a composing mood.

"For example, on one of the hottest summer days in Hollywood, at Jule Styne's request, we were attempting to write new material. It was so hot that I turned to Jule and said, 'Hey! why don't we get in my car and head out to the beach?' Typically he turned to me and said, 'Why don't we stay here and write a winter song?' Within an hour I gave him an opening line and before the afternoon ended we had written 'Let It Snow, Let It Snow,' which, of course, went on to become a yuletide standard—it's my 'White Christmas.' Later that day, inspired by the weather, we also wrote, 'The Things We Did Last Summer.'"

Born on the lower east side of New York City, June 18, 1913, he was the third child in a family of five and the only boy. His parents emigrated from their native Poland in 1905. A slight child, who wore glasses and carried a violin case, he overcame those liabilities in his rough neighborhood by being mischievous and one of "the boys."

His father operated a small restaurant and, in Sammy's own words, "We never went hungry." His mother he fondly recalled as "somebody you could make a deal with—like no more violin lessons after my Bar Mitzvah." His proficiency on that difficult instrument did win him early employment with local bands, but he soon switched to his lifelong love, the piano. Two famous comedians from his neighborhood were close friends, Phil Silvers and Milton Berle. He had two children from his first marriage, daughter Laurie and son Stephen, and he was a proud grandparent. Laurie had the thrill of accepting one of his Oscars.

Of all the show business biographies that have been written, Sammy's own story was one of the most entertaining. Taking its title from another of his hit songs, *I Should Care* was a 1974 best seller. When it was published, playwright and author Garson Kanin wrote the following: "Other times have had their minstrels and troubadours; other places their balladeers and chansonniers. We have Sammy. Not Sam, not Samuel, but indubitably Sammy. He is a party, and so is his book."

My copy of his fascinating show business story was personalized with these words: "For Elaine and Gord Atkinson—here I am between the covers, pardon the old pun! What pleasures me most is that Gordon you have me 'vocally on tape,' which is the real me? In any case on paper or on tape or in person you have my great gratitude for being a friend of words and music!"

In 1974 he also made his stage debut as a performer in his widely acclaimed one-man show, *Words and Music*. "I went on the stage for the first time formally," he told me, "at the Golden Theater and realized my dream of stepping on a Broadway stage. I wanted desperately to be a vaudevillian and finally realized my dream at age 60. For after all what is the whole point of life if you don't have a goal?" A gifted raconteur and one of the best "song demonstrators" in the business, his show took him across North America and across the Atlantic to London, where it won rave reviews.

My last interview with Sammy was at the famous Friar's Club in mid-Manhattan, where he had been a lifelong member. He ended our conversation by saying somewhat philosophically and prophetically, "General Douglas MacArthur said: 'Old soldiers never die, they simply fade away'; well, songwriters literally never die, their music keeps them here forever."

✪ ✪ ✪

...ANECDOTE

Sometimes fans will challenge celebrities about their backgrounds and even their identities. One evening when Jack Benny was leaving a Las Vegas hotel with Rich Little, a lady approached them and addressed Benny as "Mr. Burns." The mild mannered comedian could not convince her that he was not George Burns. After several minutes of frustration he asked her what her name was; when she said, "I'm Mrs. Mary Brown," Benny said with conviction, "Oh no you're not!"

"A golden moment"—celebrating world-wide sales of Paul Anka recordings, 1981.

The Times of His Life

When a young home-town entertainer becomes an international star, it sometimes seems that almost everyone in the community knew and supported him from the beginning. Paul Anka's youthful energy and driving ambition did indeed bring him into contact with a wide cross-section of early Ottawa associates and acquaintances—a few of them became lifelong friends.

In 1954 my career in broadcasting brought me from Toronto to Ottawa. My first business luncheon was at one of the capital's few superior restaurants of that era, The Locanda. It was owned and operated by the Anka family. My wife and I became frequent patrons and, before long, close friends of Paul's late parents, Andy and Camelia (who was known affectionately as Camy). It was at The Locanda that we met the eldest of their three children, who was thirteen and on occasions after school helped out in the restaurant.

With his sister Mariam and their younger brother, Andy Jr., often in tow, Paul soon became a regular visitor to my Saturday afternoon radio show, *The Campus Corner.* With two high school pals he formed a trio called The Bobbysoxers and made his broadcast debut on one of our talent programs. Paul remembers that formative time of his life fondly:

"I remember coming down to the radio station, and our early encounters with our inter-family relationship, and meeting you for the first time at the restaurant. I often reflect on my early years in Ottawa and they are very clear in my mind. I still feel my roots are there—and remember many incidents vividly, like being on the radio for the first time with you; appearing at Lansdowne Park with my trio The Bobbysoxers; my first television show from the Château Laurier Hotel, when all my friends and relatives showed up; and the bitter-sweet memory of my dear mother's shock at hearing that on my way to an engagement in neighboring Hull, I had been picked up by an RCMP officer for driving her little car without a license.

"So much has changed back home, but I still meet old friends and savor those memories with them—like several years ago seeing Diana again and sharing with her events of those formative years."

Paul was born July 30, 1941. He has been honored by his home town with the key to the city and a street bearing his name.

In the late 1950s New York was, as it is now, the center of the music industry, and Paul with youthful enthusiasm entered and won a contest for a weekend trip to Manhattan. Exposed to the recording world, he was determined to someday record one of his songs. A year later, while visiting an uncle in Los Angeles who was also a singer, he realized his dream. Full of drive and determination, he auditioned a novelty number for a producer from a small record label. The song's title was inspired by a town in South Africa with a long and fascinating name, "Bluawildebeestefontain." It was the locale of the plot of a John Buchan novel, *Prester John*, which Paul studied while at Fisher Park High School. Upon his return to Ottawa the record became a local hit. Now it's a rare collector's item among Anka fans.

Another frequent visitor to our radio broadcasts was the young lady who inspired Paul's first and biggest international hit. Diana Ayoub recalls the background to the song that made her a somewhat reluctant celebrity: "At the time I had a very close girlfriend, and Paul would travel with us around town. I was 17 and had a driver's license and access to my father's car. Paul was 15 when he wrote the song. He was very frustrated at the time, wanting to sing rather than study at school. He would enter amateur contests over in Hull, when he should have been doing homework. His father was concerned about his future, but his mother would cover for him, and I would encourage him and often drive him to these shows. I thought he was just attached to me because of the support I gave him. When he first sang the song to me I was stunned—I didn't quite know how to handle it."

"I went back to New York," Paul remembers, "and did the rounds of the record companies, but primarily to ABC-Paramount, where I wanted to meet a man who was a musical genius, the late Don Costa. After hours of waiting for an appointment I finally entered his office and auditioned my songs. To my delight, he agreed to work with me. In a sense he took these songs and gave them the professional polish and arrangements they needed, and then produced the recording sessions. The company brought my flabbergasted parents to New York, who were wondering 'What is Paul up to now?' I signed a contract, worked under Costa's guidance, and a couple of months later recorded 'Diana.'"

"In those days you recorded live with the orchestra and had no opportunity to mix and match different versions later. It was quite thrilling, and out of that one afternoon my career began as a recording artist and performer."

Paul Anka presenting me with the first copy of "Diana" to be played on the radio, circa 1957.

A short time later Paul arrived back in Ottawa and presented me with the first copy of "Diana" to be played on my radio show for his home-town fans.

Within a matter of months Paul became the first of the young jet-set performers with sold-out performances in London, Paris, Rome and Tokyo. It all happened so quickly that, like everyone else, Paul found his overnight fame overwhelming. Upon his return from his first visit to the Orient, he spent an evening at our home showing us his own movies of his tumultuous reception in Japan; he looked at the films with almost detached amazement.

The transition of Paul from a teenage recording artist to a multi-talented composer and performer began very early in his professional development. It started with his discovery of a dramatic ballad and a telephone conversation. Paul remembers that call like it really was yesterday: "I had a couple of hits at that time and I wanted to change my style to a larger orchestral texture. There was an old song that I had found in my parent's sheet music, and I called you and said, 'Gord, do you remember a song called 'All of a Sudden My Heart Sings?' You told me that it had been introduced by Kathryn Grayson in the MGM musical *Anchors Aweigh*. I thought it could be a hit for me and would appeal to both my younger fans and a more mature audience. With your encouragement I called Don Costa and arranged a recording date. I flew back to New York for the session and within a few weeks of its release the record was on the charts—and to think that one of my all-time hits, and a recording that changed my musical direction, began with a telephone call to you from the basement recreation room of my parent's Ottawa home!"

Years later I met with Broadway composer Harold Rome, who wrote the words to "All of a Sudden My Heart Sings." He was fascinated with the story behind Paul's recording, which he said he had not heard before. He also told me that Paul's version of his song had given it a new lease on life.

In 1961 Paul's transition from a teen star to an adult performer was confirmed when he was booked at Manhattan's sophisticated nightclub the *Copacabana*. His Broadway debut followed that year when he replaced a vacationing Steve Lawrence in the title role of *What Makes*

Sammy Run. He developed his skills as an actor guesting on TV dramas, which resulted in his being signed by movie mogul Darryl F. Zanuck to portray a young soldier in the sweeping cinema account of D-Day, *The Longest Day.* That assignment gave him the opportunity to write his most memorable motion picture theme.

"Coming from the music world," Paul recalled, "I was very curious who was going to write the music for the film. We were all living and filming at Caen in Normandy. Mr. Zanuck told me that he wasn't planning on having any music on the soundtrack. He didn't want anything to interrupt the authenticity of the action, or that would overscore his production. I agreed with him, but told him that I had a feeling about the film, and asked him to at least listen to a melody that I had in mind. He agreed, and after shooting was completed I went back to New York, hired a band, and spent about $5,000 on a demo of my song, which reflected everything I felt about *The Longest Day.* I sent it to him and received a telegram back which read: 'You've got it! I love it.' A few days later I met with the French arranger-composer Maurice Jarre and he scored the picture. I think about 15 minutes of the theme was used throughout the entire movie. It was another major break for me as a composer."

While performing in Puerto Rico Paul met his wife, Anne, who had a very successful career as an international fashion model. The daughter of a diplomat, Anne was born in Egypt and spent her childhood in the Middle East and France. The Ankas are the proud parents of five adult daughters, whose names all begin with the letter "A": Alexandre, Amanda, Alicia, Anthea and Amelia.

The artistic life of Paul Anka has been a double-life as an acclaimed international performer and a prolific composer. While still a teenager he wrote five songs that became number one hits, "Diana," "You Are My Destiny," "Puppy Love," "Lonely Boy" and "Put Your Head on My Shoulder." During those early years he began writing songs for other performers and has continued to do so throughout his career. His reflected hits have included Tom Jones' "She's a Lady" and Buddy Holly's "It Doesn't Matter Anymore."

"I knew Buddy Holly very well. We surfaced around the same time with 'That'll Be the Day' and 'Diana.' He was a very talented man, a distinctive sounding vocalist and guitarist, and one that many people freely took 'licks' from and learned from. I was on the same tour with him just before the tragic flight that took his life. I was aware of the planned airplane trip and had it not been full to capacity I might have been on it. The last song he recorded was one that I had written for him and ironically it was titled, 'It Doesn't Matter Anymore.' It was one of the few songs that he recorded that he hadn't written."

One of the most familiar themes written by Paul was played nightly for three decades on NBC's *Tonight Show*. "It's the one melody that I haven't combined with lyrics. It was a big money earner and a very special kind of copyright. I think it really captured Johnny Carson's personality and that late night feeling. Copyrights are so special in terms of lasting value and rewards."

When Frank Sinatra came out of his brief self-imposed retirement, his long-time lyricist Sammy Cahn collaborated with Paul on his comeback song, "Let Me Try Again." Cahn had been for many years a great influence on Paul and one of the Anka family's closest friends.

It was just prior to Sinatra's announced retirement that Paul and his family were vacationing in Europe. "We were staying in a little town in the south of France and I kept hearing a song on the radio that I liked very much. I wrote down the title, "Comme d'habitude," which means 'as usual.' On our way home we went back to Paris. I called the publisher and told him that I would like to purchase the rights to their song. He seemed very happy to give them to me for a wider audience. I brought it home and lived with it for some time.

"That same year I got to know Frank Sinatra rather well. I had always admired him and was flattered when he asked me if I would write him a farewell ballad for his retirement. One night after returning from France I was in my music room, it was pouring rain outside and I was playing with the same melody when a line came to me that seemed a perfect fit, 'and now the end is near and so I face the final curtain.' I said to myself, 'Sinatra, retirement. That's it!' I finished the lyrics with words right out of his mouth. In my mind I could hear him perform the song that he would make famous. I woke up Anne and with tears in my eyes sang to her the ballad I called 'My Way.'

"I phoned Vegas where Sinatra was playing and went out there with a piano demo. Don Costa, who was working with him, called me up and told me that they were going to record it—they rehearsed and went in fast for the session. I went back to New York and they called me the following day and played it for me on the telephone. It changed my career. It was a milestone and a turning point in my life."

A nostalgic refrain that Paul wrote for a series of Kodak radio and TV commercials extolled the importance of film memories. Its theme was reflected in its title, "The Times of Your Life." Considering his long and varied career, his charitable works and his commitment to family values, it could be his signature song or the title of his autobiography.

✪ ✪ ✪

Paul making his nightclub debut at the Copacabana, New York, 1961.

"Acting has never been the end-all for me." Don Ameche backstage at the National Arts Centre, Ottawa, 1976.

An Underrated Actor

Throughout most of his career Don Ameche was one of Hollywood's most underrated actors. Only in the latter years of his life and following his death in 1993 did the movie industry recognize his status as one of the screen's most versatile thespians. In 1986 he won the best supporting Oscar in the science fiction fantasy *Cocoon* and two years later was voted best actor at the prestigious Venice Film Festival for his amusing and sensitive performance in *Things Change*.

A thoughtful, unassuming man, Ameche was rarely a part of the Hollywood social scene. His interests were varied and his career never took precedence over his family life. Although he loved to work he was never far away from his wife, Honore, their six children, and later their thirteen grandchildren and three great-grandchildren.

"Acting has never been the begin-all and end-all for me. It's just a job I do," he told me. "I didn't associate with most actors because acting was all they ever thought about. Hank (Henry) Fonda was an outstanding actor, but he rarely talked about anything but acting. Tyrone Power was the same; however, I was probably as close to Ty as anyone."

He was christened Dominic Felix Amici in Kenosha, Wisconsin, where he was born in 1908 to an Italian immigrant couple. His father was a saloon keeper who spoke with an accent similar to the old shoeshine boy character that Don portrayed in *Things Change.*

A film actor since 1936, he decided on an acting career while attending law school. At the University of Wisconsin he appeared in a campus production of *The Devil's Disciple.* In 1929 he made his professional debut playing the role of a butler in a long-forgotten Broadway drama.

Among the films of his most productive time, the 1930s and 1940s, were memorable titles like *Alexander's Ragtime Band* with Alice Faye and Tyrone Power, *In Old Chicago* with the same co-stars, *Swanee River* (in the role of Stephen Foster) and again with Alice Faye in *The Story of Lillian Russell,* followed by *Down Argentine Way* with Betty Grable—and the movie that placed his name in the parlance of Hollywood slang, *The Story of Alexander Graham Bell.* For years after he appeared in that film account of the life of the inventor of the telephone it was common for movie-goers to refer to the telephone as "the Ameche."

I first interviewed him in 1976 on "the Ameche" from his home in Beverly Hills. By coincidence he had watched the "Bell" movie on late-night TV the previous evening. "It was a much better picture than I remembered," he told me, "and it certainly had a wonderful cast with Loretta Young and Henry Fonda sharing the billing."

Of all his early films one stands out as a classic. "*Heaven Can Wait* was my personal favorite," he recalled fondly during an in-person interview. "It was produced by the only great director I ever worked for, Ernst Lubitsch. He was an absolute genius when he was in his true métier. He really made it a memorable experience for me." The 1943 screen story followed a rake's progress as he faced his own mortality and was comforted by his one true love. Gene Tierney was his leading lady. Warren Beatty's 1978 movie had the same title, but it was a re-make of *Here Comes Mr. Jordan.*

"Sometimes when the camera is rolling, it captures something that only the camera can see. It can flatter an actor or make him look unattractive. Clark Gable in person was a rather unassuming fellow, but on the screen he was larger than life. A good director like Lubitsch could operate a camera to the full advantage of his actors."

Don Ameche was well known to radio audiences not only as the star of dramatic programs but for several years as a regular on the *Edgar Bergen & Charlie McCarthy Show.* He often played the part of a slightly shady lawyer exchanging quips with Bergen's famous dummy. Many stars who appeared on that program were so taken with Charlie's humor that they didn't think of him as a ventriloquist's prop. "I don't know if I ever thought of him as a real person. I don't know if I could have gone that far," Ameche admitted, "but to think of him only as a dummy, I don't believe I did, really."

A popular domestic radio series that was played purely for laughs, *The Bickersons*, teamed him with songstress Frances Langford. "The network had no trouble persuading me to do it, but Frances was somewhat reluctant since she had done little acting up to that point. However, once she took on the role she loved it, and we were on the air for three seasons."

In 1950 Ameche left Hollywood and returned to the New York stage, starring in two Broadway musicals, *Silk Stockings* and *Goldilocks.* In the late 1970s he had a very successful North American tour with a revival of the Vincent Youman's musical comedy, *No, No Nanette.*

In 1983 he accepted a role in the Eddie Murphy comedy *Trading Places*, which also featured another veteran actor, Melvyn Douglas. He was re-discovered by Hollywood and staged an impressive film comeback in *Cocoon* and *Things Change.* Only in those final years of his career did he win the acceptance that had eluded him throughout his life—the recognition of the critics, the public and his peers that he was indeed "an actor's actor."

The Man with the Golden Horn

In that unforgettable era when the music of the big bands filled the airwaves and swing was the thing, a mild-mannered trumpet player was acclaimed the world over as "The Man With the Golden Horn."

Harry James was one of the shining stars of that golden age and an inventive musical pioneer. His mastery of the trumpet set a standard for future virtuosos of this demanding instrument. His distinctive style was aggressive and biting on up-tempo tunes, smooth and caressing on romantic melodies. He had the innate ability to always feature the songs his fans wanted to hear and at the proper pace for every occasion.

Sometimes he changed the tempo of songs from the composer's original sheet music. Two of his biggest hits were penned by Jule Styne, but James heard them differently than the famous songwriter—he slowed down the tempo of "I Don't Want to Walk Without You" and played "I've Heard That Song Before" at a faster beat.

In the mid-1940s the Harry James Band was one of the most danceable orchestras on records, on radio and on the prestigious ballroom circuit. They appeared in Hollywood musicals and their recordings consistently appeared on the hit parade charts. Their most memorable ballad was the sentimental postwar love song "It's Been a Long, Long Time."

An active performer until late in his life, he never lost his magical trumpet touch and continued to tour until a short time before his death at 67 in 1983. I had the pleasure of meeting and interviewing him during one of his last tours.

In a manner of speaking you could say that Harry James was "born in a trunk." "My mother was an aerial performer," he told me, "who doubled as a featured vocalist. She had a lovely trained voice and performed operatic arias in what was called a spectacular act. My father was a coronet player and the circus band leader. I was born in Albany, Georgia, while the Christy Bros. Circus was midway through a 1916 tour. Just 13 days after my arrival, my mother was back performing under the Big Top. We spent our winters in Beaumont, Texas, where I received my formal education. After my folks retired from the circus, my Dad became the music director for the school board."

Young Harry's career in show business began as a four-year-old contortionist. "Well, I'll tell you, when your family is part of a circus it doesn't matter how old you are," Harry recalled, "you must do a job of some kind. By the time I was six my Dad began my musical education. I played the drums for four years with the circus band before I took up the trumpet."

During his early teens he had the opportunity to audition for Lawrence Welk. "He had a six-piece group in those early years that was billed as 'The Biggest Little Band in the West.' I auditioned for him in Dallas and he liked my playing, but was unable to hire me because all his musicians played three or four instruments. He liked to tell that story to musician friends, saying that the biggest favor he ever did for anyone was not hiring me!"

Not long after that near brush with fame, Harry won an audition with Ben Pollack's Band, a musical aggregation that featured at various times many of the famous names of the swing years. His solo work with Pollack caught the attention of Benny Goodman.

"I was only 20 when I joined Benny and was most fortunate to be with him at the famous Carnegie Hall concert of 1938. My fellow musicians were the likes of Gene Krupa, Lionel Hampton, Teddy Wilson and Ziggy Elman. It was the first time jazz had been featured in a major concert hall.

"I remained with the Goodman band for 2 years and then with Benny's help went out on my own. He loaned me $1900 and he eventually got back $20,000 for his investment!"

In the beginning the powerhouse style of the James band was ignored by the public, but following a lean period of a couple of years and a switch to mellow as well as swing music he had the song-pluggers beating a path to his bandstand. His number one hit records included "A Sleepy Lagoon," "You Made Me Love You," "I'm Beginning to See the Light," "You'll Never Know" and his theme song, "Ciribiribin." His featured vocalists all went on to solo careers: Helen Forrest, Dick Haymes, Kitty Kallen and his most famous graduate, Frank Sinatra.

"I was listening to the radio at my New York apartment one night, shortly after I formed the band, and I heard this boy singing out at a place called the Rustic Cabin, and the following evening, after we finished our show at The Paramount Theater, I went out to hear him and before I left I signed him to a year's contract at $75 a week." It was, however, a bleak time for the James crew. "The first time we were booked in California we were so poor that we would chip in a quarter each and Frank's first wife, Nancy, would make a spaghetti dinner for all of us—and that's the way we survived for the six weeks we were in Los Angeles."

One collaboration during that period launched Sinatra's career and established the Harry James Band—the haunting lament "All Or Nothing at All." "Frank eventually came to me," he recalled, "and told me Tommy Dorsey had offered him $150 a week and that Nancy was expecting a baby, and would I mind if he took the job. I told him to go with my blessing, and if things didn't work out for the band I might join him. He still owes me five months at $75 a week. Frank keeps telling me, 'any time boss, just let me know when.' He's a beautiful man."

By the early 1940s Harry's golden horn had taken him to Hollywood, where he married one of the screen's most popular stars, the blonde pin-up queen, the late Betty Grable. They worked together often in those turbulent years at camp shows for servicemen, and as late as the 1960s they were appearing as a team in Las Vegas. During the era of movie musicals he was under contract to 20th Century Fox and appeared in several films—including a surprise walk-on in a Betty Grable romantic comedy.

Benny Goodman once described Harry James as a "musical innovator and gifted musician." His fans remember him as the leader of one of the outstanding groups of "Music Makers of the Golden Age of Swing."

"The First Lady of the Stage"— My personal photograph of Helen Hayes, New York, 1987.

THE FIRST LADIES OF THE STAGE AND SCREEN

The late Helen Hayes was affectionately called "The First Lady of the American Theater." It was a title that she richly deserved. Her death in March of 1993 followed the passing of her lifelong friend, Lillian Gish, who was to the screen what Miss Hayes was to the theater, an incomparable performer. Both legendary actresses were in their nineties and active supporters of their art until the end of their remarkable lives.

Miss Gish, who was 99 at the time of her death, was Hollywood's first and most enduring star. Her pioneering career, which spanned eight decades, can never be challenged. The star of Hollywood's first epic, D.W. Griffith's *Birth of a Nation*, she last appeared before the cameras in 1989 with Bette Davis in *The Wales of August*.

Helen Hayes

When Helen Hayes succumbed to heart failure at 92, her passing was mourned by theater-goers and critics alike. She was the widow of playwright Charles MacArthur, who wrote the script for her first major film, *The Sin of Madelon Claudet*, which won her a 1931 Academy Award. Their adopted son, James MacArthur, achieved international recognition in the popular TV series *Hawaii Five-0.* Their daughter Mary died of polio at age 19, shortly before the scheduled opening of one of Miss Hayes' Broadway plays.

The Hayes anthology of outstanding theatrical performances included *Victoria Regina, Twelfth Night, The Skin of Our Teeth, The Glass Menagerie, Harvey*, and her Tony-winning roles in *Happy Birthday* and *Time Remembered.* She left the theater in 1971 due to stage dust that aggravated her chronic bronchitis. However, she continued to appear in films and on TV. A year before her theatrical retirement, she won a supporting Oscar for her role in *Airport.*

The recipient of three Tonys, an Emmy and two Oscars, the diminutive actress joined the ranks of America's nobility when she was presented the Kennedy Center's Lifetime Achievement Award by President Reagan, who also awarded her the Medal of Freedom.

I had the honor of meeting Miss Hayes at the launch of her third book at New York's Algonquin Hotel in 1987. Her previous best sellers were entitled, appropriately, *A Gift of Joy* and *Upon Reflection.*

A Manhattan landmark, The Algonquin was the home of the fabled literary "Round Table" of the 1920s, and was an appropriate setting for a cocktail party honoring a truly legendary lady. The wit and wisdom of Alexander Woolcott, Dorothy Parker, Robert Benchley and their circle of writers and humorists of that bygone era echoed through the corridors of the grand old hotel.

At the invitation of Miss Hayes' publicist, I met her just prior to the arrival of the press corps. She was as charming and sincere as I thought she would be, and in our few moments of conversation gave me her full attention.

After she autographed my copy of her new book, *Loving Life*, a lady friend she hadn't seen in many years arrived at the reception, and to my surprise she asked me if I would take pictures of them with my camera. I mailed her copies of the photos a short time later, and to my delight she returned one as a portrait, which she autographed in a very warm and personal way. The picture has a place of honor in my home with its thoughtful inscription: "To Gord Atkinson, Blessings! Helen Hayes."

...ANECDOTE

Some days are better than others on the entertainment scene. On the evening of the day in 1984 that I interviewed James Stewart, Rich Little and I with our wives and his mother dined at an Italian restaurant in Malibu. Halfway through our meal Rich whispered to me, "Gord, Cary Grant is in the booth right behind you." Of course I thought he was joking and before long would be saying, "Judy, Judy, Judy," and doing an impression of the famous actor. But then I heard a very familiar voice behind me and realized it was indeed the one and only Cary Grant. As we were leaving the restaurant, Rich introduced us to him and his wife and we had a very pleasant conversation. Once we were outside Rich couldn't resist saying to me, "How's that in one day, Jimmy Stewart and Cary Grant!"

"Rudolph" and the Man Who Made Him Famous

In 1939 Robert L. May, a young advertising agent who was a copy writer and idea man for a major Chicago department store, was asked to organize a staff Christmas party. Not content to arrange a typical social get-together he put his considerable talent and imagination into the planning. The event was a big success, and his parodies of popular songs had everyone singing along. Management was impressed with his abilities and asked him to organize the store's advertising campaign for the following yuletide.

Looking for an identifiable company symbol for the Christmas season, he thought about Santa's reindeer and a story he once read about a North Pole outcast.

"The idea for Rudolph was no flash in the night," he told reporters. "I kept thinking that my reindeer had to be an ugly-duckling type, and that the reason why he was ostracized from the herd would also have to be the reason for his eventual popularity with other reindeer. Speed and strength were hardly qualities which made for an underdog, but flying in all sorts of weather seemed to have possibilities."

May's first inclination was to give his reindeer bright eyes that would light the route for St. Nick. "As I thought of how to portray the lighted eyes," he continued, "my thoughts went from his eyes to his nose—and then I knew I had it—a bright red nose to light Santa's way in fog, mist and snow."

Nine years later a prolific composer-lyricist, Johnny Marks, immortalized May's imaginary holiday hero with a song that ranks behind only "White Christmas" as an all-time yuletide best seller.

The man who wrote the season's favorite children's ditty was 76 when he celebrated his last Christmas in 1985. I was fortunate to meet with him at his New York office in the famous Brill Building of Tin Pan Alley folklore. It was a wintry morning and a short time before his passing. He spoke in a deep Santa Claus-like voice, which I should have expected, since his music publishing company was called St. Nicholas Music.

The Marks family came from snow country, Mt. Vernon, New York, which his publicist claimed was just a reindeer ride away from the North Pole.

"I keep a big book with about 400 titles that I've heard or that have occurred to me," Marks revealed, "and when I'm looking for an inspiration I glance through the list. When I jotted down "Rudolph" I tried to fit it to a melody, but my original tune was unsatisfactory. The following year an unusual thing happened to me; as I was walking down the street from my office, I suddenly started humming a tune that seemed made to order. I went home, finished the music, dug through my notes, found my original lyrics and re-wrote them to fit the new melody."

The ultimate yuletide novelty song was rejected as being too novel by several top recording artists and was almost passed over by the famous cowboy star who made it the runaway hit of 1949.

"The song might never have happened," Marks remembered, "had it not been for unusual circumstances that brought it to the attention of Gene Autry. I had sent copies to Bing Crosby, Dinah Shore, the Andrews Sisters and other popular stars, only to have them returned, suggesting it might be more suitable for someone else. Autry got his demonstration record through the mail, and listened to it at his office. As almost an afterthought he brought it home with eight other songs, intending to pick four for his next record session.

"Several years later he told me that he had decided not to do it. He didn't think it would fit his image, since he was known for western classics like 'Tumbling Tumbleweeds' and 'South of the Border.' But his late wife Ina coaxed him to include it in the session. She thought it was the best novelty she had ever heard, and asked him to do her a favor and put it on one side of a record, and then put what he thought might be a hit on the other side. The rest, as Gene said, is musical history."

The Autry record ranks as one of the industry's few instantaneous hits. It was released in mid-September and topped the charts within a month. By Christmas it had sold over two million copies—a phenomenal accomplishment for that time. Back then the record industry seldom acclaimed even a million seller.

At the time of our interview Marks told me that the original Autry version had sold over five million copies down through the years and that all versions of "Rudolph" had amassed international sales estimated at well over fifty million records. His lyrics have been translated into every major language and his enduring and infectious melody has been performed all over the world.

"The idea that you just sit down at the piano and write a song is far from the truth," he reminded me. "Each of my songs has happened in a different way. For example, 'A Holly, Jolly Christmas' was written for the *Rudolph the Red Nosed Reindeer* TV special. That came about because the sponsor, General Electric, wanted one song for a key scene in the animated feature that would imply 'Merry Christmas' without that actual greeting. I went back to my book of titles and found the perfect substitute in 'A Holly, Jolly Christmas.' The GE people thought I was a genius and could hardly believe that almost overnight I came up with the perfect song to close the show."

The annual video romp of "Rudolph," with narration and songs performed by Burl Ives, became a Christmas tradition.

The Marks yuletide musical magic gave us two additional major holiday hits: a dramatic song set to Longfellow's famous poem "I Heard the Bells on Christmas Day," introduced by Bing Crosby, and the first seasonal success of the rock era, popularized by Brenda Lee, "Rockin' Around the Christmas Tree."

Few composers are blessed with the ability to blend words and music that capture the hearts and the imagination of people from all walks of life. They live on in their music as their songs are handed down from generation to generation. Johnny Marks was one of the gifted few.

"A vital and lively octogenarian"—Mitch Miller on stage at the National Arts Centre, May 9, 1996. The Atkinsons joined the audience to "Sing Along with Mitch."

A YANKEE DOODLE DANDY

Mitch Miller, the bearded maestro of the podium, has kept the world singing for over 40 years. His sing-along LP collections made him one of the best-selling recording artists of all time, while his TV appearances made him one of North America's most recognizable figures. His popularity as a performer, however, has overshadowed his accomplishments as an acclaimed serious musician.

"That's the power of television," he agreed, during an interview from his home in Manhattan. "On the other hand, musicians are aware of my credentials and that's much more satisfying."

He was only 11 when he began oboe lessons. "It was the only instrument left in the school lockers," he said with a smile, "when I decided to pursue music." A scholarship student at the Eastman School of Music in his native Rochester, New York, he played professionally with the Syracuse Symphony and the Rochester Philharmonic.

When he moved to New York City he played in both symphony ensembles and popular orchestras, eventually touring with George Gershwin. He has received universal acclaim for his idiomatic interpretation of Gershwin's varied works down through the years.

A friendly, vital and lively octogenarian, he is an engaging personality and entertainer. Born in 1911, on the same day as George M. Cohan, July 4, Miller has reflected almost every aspect of music during a remarkable career that has spanned over six decades and, like Cohan, has left his own mark on American music. His greatest hit was the rousing 1955 gold recording of "The Yellow Rose of Texas."

He still appears both as a performer and as a musician during his frequent engagements. As a guest conductor with symphony orchestras he features great pop orchestral favorites, and with song sheets supplied he invites his many fans to sing along.

As a record producer, Miller was one of the most influential artist and repertoire executives of the 1940s and 1950s. He introduced a unique line-up of singers and musicians to the Mercury and Columbia record labels. "It is very satisfying to know that some of the outstanding artists that I worked with back then are still at the top of their craft: Tony Bennett, Rosemary Clooney, Johnny Mathis, Vic Damone and Jerry Vale, to name only a few. I was also privileged to sign Toronto's Percy Faith and the Four Lads to contracts. I first heard Percy on a broadcast from Canada and when he arrived in New York I was his oboe player."

Not all the artists that were under his supervision at Columbia were pleased with the songs he assigned to them. Rosemary Clooney was directed to a big hit with her novelty number, "Come on-a My House," but Miller also had her record off-beat songs that she likes to forget. Frank Sinatra, toward the end of his career at Columbia, was critical of some of the songs Miller gave him to record and left the label for a Capitol Records contract and a resurgence of his career. But as Rosemary Clooney has often said, "You can't argue with success and Mitch had a lot more hits than misses."

It was in 1947 that one of the musical highlights from the Miller recording library occurred, when the great Leopold Stokowski asked him to play English horn with his world-famous orchestra. "Stokie," as Miller called him affectionately, "was a musical giant. He established Victor's classical Red Seal label. He inspired everyone who worked for him to strive for perfection. Of course, in those days if you made the slightest mistake while recording, you had to start all over again!"

While several of his vintage records have been re-issued to his satisfaction on CDs, he has not been as pleased with the handling of his sing-along LPs that are back on the market. "They haven't been packaged properly," he explained, "since they don't include the printed lyrics of the songs. Nevertheless, I am still receiving healthy royalties from them."

Another conductor and band leader who was a Miller discovery, Ray Conniff, followed in his musical footsteps. "Ray's recordings were a natural progression from our sing-along albums, which led to the swinging vocal and instrumental style he developed. He sold so many records over a 20-year span that he is still collecting impressive royalties."

While Miller had hoped that his first sing-along LP would be well received, he was astonished at its overnight success. "It came out at the height of the early popularity of rock 'n' roll, but we felt that the time might be right to hit a responsive chord with the public for a collection of old favorite campfire songs. The albums that followed repeated the success of the first release, and other artists and record companies tried to duplicate their public acceptance. But, you know, the hardest thing to do is to make something that is very simple both interesting and entertaining. We kept our presentations appealing in an old-fashioned way, and for that reason I believe they are timeless and will endure."

Mel Tormé at his home in Beverly Hills in 1974.

A Consummate Performer

Mel Tormé has been acclaimed as one of the great jazz artists of our time. Although he has always been respected as both a pop and jazz song stylist, he believes there was one concert that confirmed his credentials as a celebrated jazz performer.

"I can almost pinpoint it," he once told me, "it was at Carnegie Hall in 1977 with George Shearing and Jerry Mulligan. When that concert took place audiences, first in New York and then happily around the world, began to see that I was trying to improve, and that I was singing in the genre that I always loved and in which I felt most comfortable. Since that time life has been extremely good to me and needless to say I am very happy about it."

A few years ago on the top-rated television program *Night Court* the principal character was a zany young judge who was a jazz aficionado and a long-time fan of Mel Tormé. The actor who played that role, Harry Anderson, off screen is a serious collector of Tormé records, who attends Mel's concerts and nightclub appearances at every opportunity.

The popularity of the TV comedy series introduced Mel to young television viewers and gave him the wide audience that only a hit show can deliver. Along with his highly successful jazz concerts, his *Night Court* exposure brought about a revival of his career—not that he has ever been away from the music scene, but a revival in the sense that he was once again a household name.

During a visit to the Tormé's Beverly Hills home, Mel told me that the creator-producer of *Night Court* was also one of his fans. "When they started talking about the character Anderson was going to play, Judge Stone, Harry and the producer entered into random conversation, and found that they both had me in common, which is wonderfully flattering. The amusing gimmick on the show," Mel continued, "was that Harry and I never meet. I was on *Night Court* several times and Harry and I kept missing one another."

Melvin Howard Tormé was born September 13, 1925, in Chicago. He has long been considered a "singer's singer." His individualistic style, matchless phrasing and colorful shading enhance his mellifluous, mellow baritone.

A child performer, he wrote his first song when he was only 14. His initial success as a recording artist was as the leader of his well-remembered vocal group The Meltones. One of his favorite memories from those early years with The Meltones was accompanying his boyhood idol Bing Crosby on a Decca recording. Coincidentally, one of his more recent CD/cassettes is a collection of 16 songs made famous by Bing, whom he calls the "singer of the century."

Soon after he struck out on his own in the late 1940s, he became a great favorite of the bobby-soxers, and was affectionately called by them "The Velvet Fog." He remembered those days vividly. "Well, it was a guy named Fred Robbins who hung the name on me. I went to New York in December of 1946 to set up some club dates, having just let The Meltones go, and having decided to embark on a solo career. I arrived at the train station, and to my surprise there were hundreds of teenage girls on the platform carrying signs that read 'Welcome Velvet Fog.' I didn't know what it was all about, or that they were welcoming me.

"As it turned out, Robbins, who was a famous New York disc jockey, had taken a liking to my work and called me 'The Velvet Fog' on his broadcasts. He used some other labels on me that were kind of fun, I thought. For example, there was 'Mr. Butterscotch' and another one he used when introducing my records was 'Here's the kid with gauze in his jaws!' Incidentally, I never propagated 'The Velvet Fog.' As a matter of fact, I would go to a town and it would be on the billboards, despite the fact that it was never stipulated in a contract. Consequently when I was able to supersede the bobby-soxers' era as an adult performer, I went to great lengths to squash it. But it was so set in the public consciousness it wouldn't go away. I still make jokes about it in my act."

Few performers have as many interests as Mel. An avid reader, who is one of the most articulate spokesmen in show business, he is fascinated with words and has a great love of languages. He is certainly the most knowledgeable movie buff I know, with an encyclopedic mind for old movies. I once watched a film in his private screening room and was amazed when he named every character actor in the picture. He is a gun collector and an authority on the old west. He has always been fascinated with aviation and is a licensed pilot. For relaxation he enjoys assembling model airplanes.

It was Mel who was instrumental in Rich Little getting his big break in Hollywood on Judy Garland's 1964 television variety show. Mel was the choral director on the program, and a frequent guest. He wrote a book about his year-long experiences with the troubled and temperamental star, *The Other Side of the Rainbow.* He followed that with his first novel, *Wynner*, the story of a big band singer. Then he completed a well-written autobiography, *It Wasn't All Velvet*, which candidly reveals the ups and downs of his personal life and career. Now happily married, he has found the contentment of domesticity which escaped him in the past.

As a songwriter Mel's name will live on for generations to come. He was only 20 when he and his friend Bob Wells wrote a Christmas ballad that has remained so popular that it has almost taken on the status of a folk song. I've always felt that Mel's own recording of that lovely yuletide song was one of the best, but my opinion is not shared by Mel himself: "I appreciate the nice words about my record, but I don't happen to think my record is very good. The first record of 'The Christmas Song,' by the man who was our inspiration, Nat 'King' Cole, was for my dough the definitive record, not mine.

"Bob Wells and I wrote the song on one of the hottest days I can remember in July, at the home of Bob's parents in Toluca Lake, California. It was too late to get the song out that year, so it wasn't released until 1946—Nat's record was released that October. We just kept thinking about a title," Mel recalled, "we were going to call it 'Merry Christmas to You,' which is the last line of the song, which seemed a little prosaic. Then we called it 'Chestnuts Roasting on an Open Fire,' which incidentally was its title for two years, because people never identified it as 'The Christmas Song.' Then the publishers combined both phrases, and it read on the sheet music 'Chestnuts Roasting on an Open Fire,' and in parentheses 'Merry Christmas to You'—and then under that the eventual title."

As is often the case with songwriters, neither Mel nor Bob Wells had any idea that they had written a song that would endure, and certainly had no premonition that it would become a Christmas classic.

"None whatsoever," Mel admitted, "we were just as delighted and surprised as everyone else when it kept getting bigger and bigger. Every Christmas for several years our publishers would tell us that ten or perhaps twenty new recordings of 'The Christmas Song' were being released. It was incredible—and new versions are still being recorded. In 1975 the copyright ran out, and we made a deal with our publishers, who have been very good to us, whereby Bob and I share in the publishers' royalties as well as all of the writers' royalties. Candidly, it has been an annuity for us and a trust fund for our children. Every yuletide we reflect back on our good fortune as the writers of 'The Christmas Song' and count our blessings."

Looking over Vincent Price's shoulder at his *Treasury of American Art.* A rare photo of him without his moustache, 1980.

AN ACTOR'S ACTOR

Although Vincent Price was an actor of great sensitivity and scope, his films with horror specialists like Boris Karloff, Peter Lorre and Bela Lugosi have typecast him in Hollywood as a very spooky character actor. While he often said jokingly, "I'm very big at Halloween!"it was an image he accepted, but one that did not do justice to his impressive body of work.

Actor, author, lecturer, art collector and gourmet cook, this multi-talented man was, as I suspected, a charming and gracious host, and a fascinating person to interview. When we first met he was appearing in his critically acclaimed one-man show as Oscar Wilde. For his performance as the great literary figure he had to shave off his moustache. Without his familiar trade mark, he told me that off-stage he often went unrecognized while touring across North America and overseas.

Mr. Price looked lightly at most of the horror movies he made and considered them to be nothing more than escapist entertainment: "I've always thought they were hysterical and comedic in a way. The ones I liked the most were *Theater of Blood* and *The Pit and the Pendulum*; they were really comedies, as was *The Raven*, which incidentally had no story at all. When Boris, Peter and I read the script we wondered what we were going to do to make it come off. So we played it for laughs and it was a lot of fun satirizing Edgar Allan Poe. One of the first 3-D pictures, *House of Wax*, was also enjoyable and quite a technical challenge for everyone."

Vincent Price was born May 27, 1911, in St. Louis, Missouri. A graduate of Yale University and the University of London (where he majored in art), he went on to study acting in England and made his London debut in a West End play. His commanding stage presence caught the attention of the producers, who before long gave him the prize part of Prince Albert in *Victoria Regina*, which he repeated in 1935 on the New York stage.

"In the theater," he recalled, "I've done over two hundred plays. Probably the best role I've ever had was appearing as Oscar Wilde. The two main plays I did on Broadway were marvelous experiences, *Victoria Regina* with Helen Hayes, which ran for three years, and *Angel Street*, one of the best psychological melodramas of all time."

During his early years in New York as a member of Orson Welles' famous Mercury Players, he began his long and varied career in broadcasting. His credits span more than six decades from *Lux Radio Theatre* to the host of the BBC's *TV Mystery Theatre*. "In radio alone I worked on over 2000 shows. I was featured in a crime series for several years, *The Saint*, and loved doing it. It was wonderful fun trying to figure out how many ways he could be hit over the head and survive for the next episode. One radio play I did had one of the best scripts ever written, a dramatization of Poe's *Three Skeleton Keys*. It's considered a radio classic today.

"I was quite active in the early days of live television on dramatic shows like *Fireside Theater* and *Hallmark Hall of Fame*, and appeared on dramatic, variety and entertainment programs of all kinds over the years. But what has kept me in a different vein and balanced my work was guesting on the big radio and TV comedy shows. I made frequent appearances with Jack Benny and had a long association with Red Skelton."

A movie called *Service de Luxe* served as the 1938 film debut of the varied and impressive film career of Vincent Price. "It was during the period," he recalled, "when many of the great silent screen stars had failed to make the transition to sound. So the studios looked for stage actors who could speak lines and project their voices. Basil Rathbone and I were among the many New York actors who answered the call of Hollywood. Since that time I've been cast in about 105 movies. My favorites were *Laura, Dragonwych, The Keys of the Kingdom,* and working for C.B. DeMille in *The Ten Commandments.* But I believe *Laura* was as close to a classic as any movie I've appeared in—Otto Preminger made it with a classical touch. The score is as haunting today as it was back in 1944."

As a respected art collector, connoisseur of good food and renowned actor, he enjoyed a series of successes as a best-selling author. His first release, *A Treasury of Great Recipes,* was followed by *A Treasury of American Art* and a fascinating book he co-authored with his son Barrett, *Man and the Monster Image.*

He and his wife, Carol Browne, met during the filming of *Theater of Blood* in 1973 and have toured together and shared billing on the London stage.

The gentle soft-spoken star who helped elevate the "horror film" to a cinema art form was increasingly alarmed by the horrors of modern living: "Horror to me is realism—the reports in our newspapers and on radio and TV, reflecting today's world. We realize that villains are seldom born but are created by our society. It is a frightening fact that some of our cities are so violent that you cannot walk alone on the street. It is a sad and terrible commentary, but that is real horror—the reports of everyday events. But for all that I am still an optimist and do believe that man's divine guidance assures us that good does eventually overcome evil."

Vincent Price passed away as a result of lung cancer, October 25, 1993.

"A Beloved Clown"—Red Skelton and I holding one of his famous clown paintings for the camera, 1989. (Photo by Paul Latour)

A Beloved Clown

Red Skelton is a show business institution. The lovable clown has brought laughter to the world for over six decades. Now in his eighties, he has dazzled his audiences in recent years with his energy, stamina and joyful outlook on life, and he intends to continue performing as long as the sound of applause enriches his life.

"I can never understand why people would work all their lives to perfect something, then when they've almost perfected it," he laments, "they retire. I can't afford to retire; I have a government to support."

Skelton is an inspiration to his contemporaries to keep as active as they can, and to live life to its fullest. His warm personality, good nature and unique sense of humor never fail to "light up a room" and make anyone fortunate enough to be in his company feel that their life has been enhanced by his presence. "I love to see people smile," he happily admits. "My work is my hobby, it's my life!" His once-familiar red hair has turned to gray, but his sense of humor has never been sharper. Commenting on his thinning locks he tells everyone, "for me, there's no more 'Head and Shoulders'—it's 'Mop and Glo.'"

I first met the multi-talented star of vaudeville, radio, movies and TV in 1966 and I was privileged to interview him again, 23 years later, when he took his one-man show on tour. He was brilliant, as he captivated theater-goers of all ages with his comedy routines, jokes, anecdotes and pantomime sketches. As a pantomimist he is world renowned—one of his biggest fans is Marcel Marceau. At every performance the audience requests that his radio and TV characters, Clem Kadiddlehopper, Freddie the Freeloader, Willy Lump-Lump, Junior, The Mean Widdle Kid and Gertrude and Heathcliff the Sea Gulls, make an appearance. The laughter of that evening in 1989 is still ringing in my ears.

(Incidentally, it was everybody's favorite mom, Harriet Hilliard Nelson, who was "Junior"'s long-suffering mother and for a time her real-life husband, Ozzie, was the Skelton show's band leader.)

Red was born into poverty July 18, 1913, two months after his father's death; his mother provided for her family by working as a charwoman in a vaudeville theater. Red's interest in entertaining began at the tender age of five, when his mother took him and his three brothers to a stage show. "I saw how the comedian made everyone laugh, and I wanted to be a clown and make people laugh."

Richard Bernard "Red" Skelton was only ten years old when he joined a medicine show, then moved on to tent shows, minstrel reviews, circuses, Mississippi showboats and burlesque, developing his comedy creations along the way. "I was a clown right from the start. My father was a circus clown while working his way through college. Clowns have great depth. Just by their expression they can look into your soul. They have an understanding of their fellow man that shines through. My father, whom I never saw, was a clown and worked in the circus during the summer while attending college. Many great performers were wonderful clowns. Two who immediately come to mind are Charlie Chaplin and Harold Lloyd; they were not just comedians, they were clowns. Comedians use topical humor and jokes to get laughs, while a clown studies his subject and gives depth and motion to people."

An accomplished artist, his paintings include still life and landscapes, and the popular Skelton Clowns which are his specialty. His original paintings sell in excess of $50,000 and are in the collections of world-famous celebrities. His series of over 40 clowns has raised large sums of money for worthy causes. Prints of these sought-after paintings have been widely circulated.

An ecumenical entertainer, he has worked tirelessly for religious organizations and charitable works. A thirty-third degree Mason, he has had private audiences with three Popes, attended command performances for Queen Elizabeth, and entertained eight U.S. presidents. He has known great personal tragedy, losing both his only son, Richard, to leukemia, and his second wife, Georgia, to depression. His dedication to comedy has sustained him and given him a purpose in life. Laughter has always been his best medicine. "God's children and their happiness are my reasons for being," he once said.

An outgoing person, he enjoys meeting people and conversing with his long-time fans. While walking with me along a busy street, on our way to a press conference, he took great pleasure when people recognized him and gave everyone a smile and a friendly "hello."

His accomplishments are many: a record 20 consecutive years as a television headliner; a comedy star of the Golden Age of Radio; top billing in 48 motion pictures; a successful career as a prolific writer of short stories, full-length books and children's stories; and a respected composer of acclaimed melodies and symphonies, performed by Arthur Fiedler, Van Cliburn and the London Philharmonic. "Some of my music is serious," he says, "but there's a little bit of whimsy in all of it."

Of his intricate schedule he insists that "You have to learn to use time, and not let it use you. I only sleep a few hours a night. The rest of the time I paint or write music or children's books." He is up at 5:30 a.m. writing and composing, and every morning when he is on the road, he writes a love letter to his wife.

While he is a fan of young comedians like Jay Leno and Robin Williams, he regrets that some of today's comedians sprinkle profanity and off-color jokes into their acts. "I think they take shortcuts in thinking. I don't think people should have to pay money to hear something they can read on bathroom walls. I'd rather hear people say, 'Boy, he was hokey!' than be turned off by questionable material."

No one laughs louder at Skelton's material than Red himself. "People always ask me why I laugh at my own jokes. I say, why should I be the only one in the hall with a straight face?"

...ANECDOTE

Once when flying to Los Angeles from Las Vegas I found myself among an all-star passenger list. On board were Orson Welles, Eddie Albert, Red Buttons, Jimmy Stewart and Rich Little. As we flew over the stark foreboding desert, Rich leaned over to me and said, "Do you realize that if this plane should crash you won't even be mentioned. And if you are identified they will probably misspell your name!"

The Mills Brothers (left to right) Herbert, Donald and Harry, at the Flamingo Hotel, Las Vegas 1974. (My jacket was brighter than the neon lights.)

The Inimitable Mills Brothers

A review of popular music of the 20th century would not be complete without a chapter dedicated to a peerless vocal group from the little town of Piqua, Ohio. For longevity and global popularity, no group of singers or musicians is more deserving of a place in musical history than the Mills Brothers.

A remarkable quartet of the 1930s and 1940s, who eventually became a trio, remained international favorites for 57 years, until the death in 1981 of one of their two lead singers, Harry Mills. A diabetic, who late in life was almost sightless, Harry was led on stage by his brothers, while their audiences were seldom aware of his handicap.

I will never forget the first time I attended a Mills Brothers' performance—the moment the famous men of harmony stepped on stage at the Flamingo Hotel in Las Vegas, the audience gave them a standing ovation.

A charge of electricity went through the room as they began their show with a driving, swinging version of the big band hit "Opus One." I was privileged to meet them backstage, following their flawless performance.

Herbert began our interview by recalling fondly their first recording session, which produced "Tiger Rag," their most enduring hit song. "We made that in 1929 in a little town in Indiana while we were appearing on a local radio station, and about two months later we left for New York and a booking on Broadway!"

In 1924, while they were still in their teens, a local Ohio band leader took them along for a radio audition in Cincinnati. The boys were such a hit that they were signed to a contract on the spot. On their broadcasts they were introduced as either "Four Boys and a Guitar" or "Four Boys and a Kazoo," until one evening they performed without the kazoo.

"Our oldest brother, John, who played guitar, reached into his pocket for the kazoo, and realized that he had left it back in our dressing room," Herbert told me. "So he tried to imitate the kazoo, and it sounded so good that we started imitating other instruments. We loved the Duke Ellington Band, and eventually tried emulating their sound with our aural impressions of the trumpet, trombone, saxophone, clarinet, bass fiddle—just about every instrument in the orchestra." For years thereafter radio listeners were convinced that the Mills Brothers were accompanied by a full complement of musicians.

John Jr., who was the oldest brother and the bass in the group, died of pneumonia at the height of their early popularity. Herbert was the next oldest, followed by Harry and Donald. Grief-stricken, the boys decided to disband the act.

"That was January 1936, and we decided to give up the act," Herbert remembered. "Our mother told us that we shouldn't quit and that John would want us to carry on. In his memory we eventually began auditioning bass singers, but none of them worked out. Then our father arrived in New York, where we were living, and said, 'Move over boys, I'm coming in!' We rehearsed with him for about two weeks, and then went right back out on the road." From that time on the famous foursome could have been billed as The Mills Family.

"Our father and mother taught us to sing and harmonize; they both had exceptional voices, and for several years traveled with a light opera company. Dad and three of his brothers were singing barbers, so barbershop harmony was taught to us early in life."

In the late 1930s the Mills men made their first overseas tour, which led to their eventual global popularity. Upon their return to New York, they discovered that during their absence the North American showbiz scene had passed them by. However, in the early 1940s they made an impressive comeback, and their popularity at home and abroad never wavered in the years that followed.

"1944 was the most amazing year for us," Harry recalled. "We had four big records that put us right back on top, 'Till Then,' 'You Always Hurt the One You Love,' 'I'll Be Around' and our biggest selling hit, 'Paper Doll.' Our earlier records like 'Lazy River,' 'Basin Street Blues' and 'Tiger Rag' would also qualify as gold records, but no one authenticated record sales back then."

John Mills Sr. died in 1968, 14 years after he left the group. At the time of his retirement, his sons decided to continue to perform as a trio—with guitar accompaniment. Happily they were able to maintain the same distinctive close harmony that had made them famous.

In the early 1930s the Mills boys often shared a microphone with Bing Crosby. They began their recording and radio careers at the same time, and had a similar impact on the development of popular music. "It was like we were made for one another," Herbert said, "Bing was weaned on jazz and did a lot of scat singing in those days, and so did my youngest brother, Donald. We made a few memorable records with Bing, including 'My Honey's Loving Arms,' 'Dinah' and 'Shine.' We were on his radio show for over eight months."

While reflecting the changing times in their repertoire, the Mills Brothers never changed their distinctive style and unmistakable harmonic blend. They had imitators, but no group could duplicate the quality of their voices and their tight harmony.

Donald, the youngest brother, who is keeping the "sound" alive singing duets with his son John, put it best when he said: "A number of trios and quartets have come to us and told us that they tried to imitate us, but they couldn't get the tonal quality. It's hard to explain, but

I think it's unique because of the closeness of the family."

The Mills Brothers' place in popular music is secure in the hearts of their countless fans, and in the accomplishments of their unparalleled career.

...ANECDOTE

With a microphone and a portable tape recorder I've been able to conduct radio interviews in places where a television crew could not enter. In 1974 while working on the *Crosby Years* series, I had an appointment to meet with Peggy Lee at her home in Beverly Hills. Although she was recovering from minor surgery, she was quite anxious to talk about her friendship with Bing. When I arrived at her house I was escorted by her housekeeper into her bedroom where she was lying in bed knitting. While I sat on a chair beside her bed she reminisced about her years with Bing on his radio shows. I was very impressed with her thoughtfulness. It was a real example of how "the show must go on."

Mel Blanc's Hollywood office, 1976, with the brass figurines of his cartoon characters in the background.

"That's All, Folks"—The Many Voices of Mel Blanc

March 20, 1984, was a most unusual day for the world-famous Smithsonian Institute of Washington, D.C. At a press reception on that date, attended by the public, an impressive and lengthy list of inductees were given formal recognition by the curators of the Smithsonian. The familiar names included Bugs Bunny, Porky Pig, Yosemite Sam, Tweetie Pie and Sylvester, the Roadrunner, Daffy Duck, Elmer Fudd, Pepe Le Pew, Woody Woodpecker, and memorable Jack Benny personalities including his railroad announcer, his violin teacher, Professor Leblanc, and even his wise-cracking parrot "Polly."

Only one elderly gentleman accepted the great honor bestowed on those fictional figures by the Smithsonian, the creator of the voices of all those characters, the incomparable Mel Blanc. Surrounded by reporters, museum officials and fans of all ages, he remembered fondly his early days in show business, and the origins of his prolific personalities which are indelibly imprinted on the aural consciousness of four generations.

During one of my most memorable trips to California, among the famous Hollywood voices that I recorded for my radio program was that kindly, warm man who gave voices to more original characters than any other person in the history of the entertainment business. I met with Mel Blanc on a summer afternoon in 1976 at his office in a highrise building in Beverly Hills, where he and his impressionist son, Noel, had a very successful commercial recording company.

Despite a near fatal automobile accident several years before, at the time of our interview he was in good spirits and seemed to be fully recovered from his many injuries.

Born in San Francisco in 1908 and raised in Portland, Oregon, young Mel was a class clown in his grammar school days. "I'd entertain the kids and get big laughs from the students and teachers—and then they would give me lousy marks. I loved music, and in high school studied a most unusual combination of instruments, violin and tuba." This led to his first job in show business, as a member of a 1927 staff radio orchestra in Portland. A short time later at 22, he became the youngest musical director in vaudeville, when he conducted the Orpheum Theater Orchestra.

When the "talkies" spelled the death knell of the old "two-a-day," he moved to San Francisco and then on to Los Angeles in a vain search for work. Returning to Portland, he made a modest living doing voices and dialects for local radio commercials. Despite the uncertainties of the Depression he and his girlfriend, Estelle, decided to face the future together and were married in 1933.

Determined to make show business his life, and with the encouragement of his bride, he returned to southern California. His ability to create voices for radio brought him to the attention of the then fledgling cartoon companies. His first movie assignment was for a man named Schlezinger, who was related to the Warner Brothers, and who needed a voice to match the antics of a drunken bull. Mel's impression ended with an ad lib, "Pass the sour mash." Schlezinger was so impressed with his ingenuity and off-beat sense of humor that he had Mel match voices with other animated characters. Within a short time Warner Brothers signed him to a contract and his unique career began.

The first of the famous voices in the amazing Blanc repertoire was inspired by a timid little cartoon pig. Mel, with tongue-in-cheek, told me that he went to a pig farm for inspiration and began talking with a grunt. The high-pitched stammering voice of Porky Pig was soon delighting children and adults alike. Porky's familiar sign-off was the inspiration for the title of Mel's autobiography, *That's Not All, Folks*. Rich Little wrote the foreword. My copy was signed, "Eh, what's up Gordon? Best regards, Bugs Bunny & Mel Blanc."

The following year, he was introduced to another animated animal that was the inspiration for his most popular and recognizable sound-track voice. Here's Mel's own recollection of that meeting: "They showed me this rabbit, and I think he was going to be called Happy Rabbit. He was the creation of a man named Bugs Hardaway. So I went to Mr. Schlezinger and suggested that they call him Bugs Bunny, as a nice way of recognizing Hardaway. Everyone liked the idea, because it was also a cute-sounding name. But they envisioned this character as a tough little guy—a real stinker. So I tried to think of a voice that would be tough, but still match a small rabbit. I experimented with speech patterns from Brooklyn and the Bronx; and then I thought, why don't I combine both New York accents, so I did, and it was easy then to coin Bugs' familiar expression, 'What's Up, Doc?'

"After that they showed me pictures of a little tiny bird and a big sloppy cat, and I gave them voices, and Tweetie Pie and Sylvester were born." In fine form Mel repeated their familiar exchange: "I taught I saw a puddy cat!"—"You did, that puddy cat is me, sufferin' succotash!" Then he recalled how the other characters developed: "They would give me a picture of a cartoon figure, like Woody Woodpecker or Speedy Gonzales, and I would come up with a voice to fit the image. Yosemite Sam was a challenge. He was a little guy, and they told me he had to be noticed, so I gave him a big rough booming voice."

Mel Blanc also left his aural imprint on television, creating original voices for video series and specials, including Barney Rubble on *The Flintstones*. While his early creations came off the drawing boards of

Warner Brothers' cartoonists, his voices brought them to life and gave them their personalities.

Of equal importance to his career was his role as a regular member of the cast of the never-to-be-forgotten Jack Benny radio and television shows. In the parlance of show business, no one could "break up" the famous comedian with greater ease than the soft-spoken impressionist.

"Jack connected me with animal sounds. On the old radio show he had a bear in his basement guarding his vault. Carmichael the bear had never uttered a sound, so Jack called me in and asked me if I could do the growl of the bear. He was so pleased with my impression that I was booked on the show the following week. That was in 1939. Well, I did the growl of the bear for six months, and that was all I did. Finally, I walked up to him and said, 'You know, Mr. Benny, I can also talk.' Well, Jack started pounding the table and fell down laughing, as he usually did when something struck him as being very funny. He said he would have the writers come up with something. But on the next program all I did was the whinny of an English horse in a comedy sketch from a race track!"

The years on the Benny program were among Blanc's happiest times. "He had a parrot," he recalled, "that couldn't talk on cue, so he asked me if I could imitate it—which I did, ending every line with, 'Look at the cheapskate!' Well Jack loved it. By the way, he could never read his lines without laughing when I did the sound of his ancient Maxwell car starting up.

"Whenever Jack went to the railway station to take an imaginary trip, I was his train caller, announcing over the public address system: 'Train leaving on track five for Anaheim, Azusa and Kookamunga.' A lot of people wrote to us and wondered how we came up with those crazy names for towns, and when we'd write back and tell them that they were the names of real California communities, they were still sceptical."

Among the many routines that Mel featured with Jack Benny, perhaps the funniest was the repetitive "Cy, Si" exchange—only a few words were spoken, but it never failed to delight audiences. "Jack was a wonderfully kind man," Mel told me, "who, unlike his public image, was very generous and most thoughtful to co-workers and fans alike."

During my visit to his office I was fascinated by a set of brass figurines of his cartoon characters that were a gift from one of his artisan friends. I took a commemorative photo of Mel standing in front of the collection, and then he thoughtfully had his secretary take a shot of both of us admiring the unique metal miniatures.

Mel Blanc passed away July 10, 1989, from heart failure; his wife of 56 years, Estelle, and his son Noel were by his side. His last recorded words (for a commercial) were taped the day before he was hospitalized. Ironically, they were Porky Pig's last words from every Warner Brothers cartoon, "That's All, Folks!"

...ANECDOTE

Following the recording of an interview I immediately check the tape recorder to make certain that the machine functioned properly. However, it was a strange procedure to follow after one unique interview. I had taped a lengthy conversation with the famous mime, Marcel Marceau. When I returned to the studio I switched tapes and gave my technician a blank cassette. A few minutes later he called me and with great concern said: "There's nothing on this tape!" to which I replied: "Well, what did you expect from Marcel Marceau?"

Guy Lombardo—April 1977—
his final tour.

GUY LOMBARDO FOR AULD LANG SYNE

Life Magazine, in a pictorial tribute to a legendary band leader which was published a short time before his passing, made this warm observation: "If Guy Lombardo did not play 'Auld Lang Syne' on New Year's Eve, a strange stillness would cover the land."

The death of London, Ontario's most famous son November 5, 1977, at 75, brought to a close the career of a musician whose popularity spanned five decades. Following funeral services near his home in Freeport, New York, attended by friends from all walks of life, including Sammy Kaye, Freddy Martin and Phil Harris, the Royal Canadians left for a performance in Massachusetts. Their press agent said: "Guy never missed an engagement in 50 years, and the band members wanted to continue the tradition."

Earlier that year Lombardo and the Royal Canadians celebrated their golden anniversary on a June evening in Port Stanley, Ontario, where the band's unique sound was first heard in 1927.

Despite the fact that the unmistakable Lombardo sound hardly changed through the years, its popularity never diminished. Over 200 million recordings by the Royal Canadians were purchased by appreciative fans, making their leader the number one salesman of the big band era.

My last interview with Lombardo was in connection with the band's 50th anniversary—it was a time for reminiscing. "We were fortunate to make our debut in the early days of radio," he stated. "By 1929 radio was no longer a novelty, having switched from battery operated to all-electric sets. With a great increase in sales, radio came alive overnight, and the bands and performers of that era took advantage of its fast-growing audience. So there is a lot of luck in this business, and timing is everything."

It was a Chicago newspaper reviewer who gave the band the most identifiable slogan in the music business. "After we had established ourselves in Chicago, and it was quite a miracle, because it happened overnight, they put us into the Palace Theater. That was the big time in those days, and Ashton Stevens of *The Tribune* was considered the top critic in town. Luckily for us, when he heard the band he began his column the following day by writing, 'Truly the sweetest music this side of heaven,' and of course that kind of stuck.

"While the theaters were important," Guy continued, "the big bands made their reputations in the hotels. They didn't make much money from the hotels, but were paid high fees for the radio broadcasts from the hotel ballrooms."

The Lombardo Orchestra was a family affair. Guy's brothers, Carmen, Victor and Lebert were prominent members of the band. Carmen was also a successful songwriter, and in collaboration with Gus Cahn and Johnny Green, wrote the first Lombardo hit ballad, "Coquette." Several of his songs made the hit parade, and one of his novelty numbers, "Boo Hoo," was a Lombardo standard.

Guy's sisters were also members of the famous musical organization for many years. Rosemarie, the youngest of the seven children born to immigrant Italian parents, was a featured vocalist with the band until she married and retired. Sister Elaine married the orchestra's very popular song stylist Kenny Gardner, and together they traveled extensively with the band.

The Lombardos' father was a tailor by trade, who was also an accomplished musician and music lover. He was responsible for his sons' musical training, and was a strict disciplinarian regarding their lessons.

Guy formed his first band from a group of neighborhood boys when he was only eleven. After graduating from high school he worked for a brief time as a bank clerk, but soon decided he would rather make music than make money—within a few years he was doing both.

In 1921 he put together his first professional organization, The Lombardo Brothers Orchestra. A perfectionist throughout his life, he refused engagements outside the London area for three years, until he felt they were ready to tour. An extended booking that began in 1924 in Cleveland, Ohio, established the Lombardo sound. That distinctive mellow sound was the musical foundation of the enduring popularity of the Lombardo entertainment dynasty.

"I'd say so," Guy agreed. "The sound is the most important thing we have, and that's God-given; you just happen to have it, like Bing Crosby's voice and Tommy Dorsey's trombone. That and our insistence on taking the pronounced beat out of the music. My brothers Carmen and Lebert play the lead, they don't listen for the drummer's beat. When we get new musicians in the band they keep listening for the drummer, but his beat is in the background—it's a subtle beat."

In a changing world the Lombardo sound was a constant. Despite the popularity of other forms of musical expression, Guy resisted the temptation of change. "We had it all our own way in the early 1930s," he admitted, "then Benny Goodman came along and was a big hit. At first we thought we would have to adapt our sound, but luckily we didn't, because Benny had his listeners and we had ours. Then along came Glenn Miller, the Dorseys, and other bands, but we all had our own following. So there is a style and audience for all kinds of music, whether it's opera, rock, swing or jazz; there's room for everyone."

While maintaining their identifiable sound the orchestra also stressed versatility, which also contributed to their long-lasting popularity. The band's charts included everything from novelty numbers to western, Hawaiian and Latin American favorites.

Guy's image as a dispenser of easy listening music was in sharp contrast to his reputation as a speedboat racer. His passion for the dangerous sport seemed like a contradiction to his gentle personality. Behind the wheel of his 30-foot hydroplane, The Tempo VII, he became a U.S. National Champion, and only quit racing in 1949 following an accident.

In 1929 the Lombardos began one of the longest associations of any orchestra in the hotel business, when they opened at the Roosevelt Hotel in New York. For nearly four decades the place to be on December 31 was the ballroom of the Roosevelt Hotel, where Guy Lombardo authenticated New Year's Eve.

Music in the Lombardo manner was also a tradition at Atlantic City's Steel Pier, and at Jones Beach, Long Island, where Guy also produced Broadway musicals during the summer holidays.

In his home town the Lombardo tradition continued after his death with a museum to his memory and an annual Big Band Festival, which attracted fans from across North America.

Guy on several occasions said that it was always an extra special pleasure to perform in the land of his birth, and especially in the London area, where his musical roots were nurtured and lasting friendships began. His place in the musical heritage of the 20th century is secure, and as long as "Auld Lang Syne" rings out an old year and brings in a new year, he will be remembered—for he was indeed a "Royal Canadian."

"The Great Dane" of comedy and music, Victor Borge, in a rare "serious moment" during a 1982 interview.

THE COURT JESTER OF THE CONCERT STAGE

Victor Borge is that rarest of all performers, a unique entertainer who is a show business original. No one has ever combined comedy and music in the theatrical manner of the man the critics acclaimed as the "Great Dane." For close to 60 years he has brought joy and laughter to international audiences with his wit and piano artistry; he is a treasured icon of the concert world.

In 1953 Borge developed his now famous one-man show, *Comedy in Music*. He has given over 5000 live performances and entertained millions of fans on TV specials, comedy recordings and the pages of his best-selling book, *My Favorite Intermissions*.

Each time I have met with him he has been a gracious and amusing host and a delightful star to interview.

"What I do on stage is what I do off stage," he once told me, "present myself the way I see situations, and the way I react to them. Of course I didn't do any comedy during my years of concertizing. However, I always thought that the restrictions of the concert stage were artificial. I thought it was a shame that a great performer like Artur Rubinstein, who was blessed with a wonderful sense of humor, was not able to express his witty observations to his audiences or comment on his music.

"What I do is nothing that I have created, so to speak, but just a natural reaction to the formality of the stage, which can be deadly, and to observations I have made on life in general."

Under the watchful eye of his mother, he was introduced to the piano at the tender age of three. His father was the first violinist with the Royal Danish Symphony. As a child prodigy of eight he made his concert debut in Copenhagen.

In the years before World War II he was already an established pianist throughout Scandinavia. He turned to comedy one night when he took the place of the star comic in a variety show who suddenly fell ill.

During the dark days of the rise of Hitler, the Borge brand of humor was a powerful weapon against the Nazi party, to such an extent that his well-being was at times in jeopardy.

"A few years before I left Denmark, there was a small Nazi party that distributed a weekly newspaper and my picture often accompanied their denunciation of my stage comments. I was ridiculing the Nazis with jokes like 'What's the difference between a dog and a Nazi?—A Nazi lifts his arm.' I also suggested that Hitler and his henchmen could sleep soundly after they signed a non-aggression pact with little Denmark. So I became a target for Nazi sympathizers. One day while out walking I was attacked by a group of hooligans. Fortunately I was light on my feet and landed a few good blows and then outraced them.

"Then I went to Sweden and took engagements in Stockholm, because I saw what was coming and wanted to prepare for the future."

The last passenger ship that left Northern Europe for North America, just prior to the U.S. entry into the war, brought American citizens and displaced persons to New York. The American consul general in Stockholm, an early Borge fan, gave a special permit to young Victor to board the ship—with this encouraging endorsement: "I hope you will make the American people laugh as much as my wife and I did at your performance."

Borge's arrival in New York was as a refugee with limited funds and little command of the English language. "I took English grammar in school, but I learned to speak the language by attending the movies. I would sit through a double bill at one of the cinemas on 42nd Street, and stay as long as I wanted for just 15 cents. I would see the same scenes over and over again, and consequently was able to absorb the language and the way that audiences responded to the dialogue. In my room I would memorize the lines and react to them—and in that way I broadened my English vocabulary."

It was from his early attempts at writing in English that he developed his hilarious punctuation comedy routine.

In 1941 he was hired to do the "warm-up" on radio's most popular variety program, *Bing Crosby's Kraft Music Hall.* He soon became a member of the famous radio cast and remained with the show for 56 weeks. "At rehearsals, Bing would come in and laugh at my routines. It was always a very friendly and casual time with him. He made you relax and feel at ease." Interestingly, in 1943 he made his movie debut in Frank Sinatra's first film, *Higher and Higher.*

Victor Borge has been given the music world's most prestigious honors and been knighted by his native Denmark, and by Sweden, Norway and Finland.

Away from his touring and international acclaim, the famous octogenarian performer is happiest when he and his wife, Sanna, entertain the families of their five children, who have given them nine grandchildren.

Born in 1909, and at this writing in his late eighties, he is still fascinated by the world around him and energized by the laughter of his audiences. "What I do is universal. Anyone who knows anything about music recognizes what I am satirizing. I have always found that a smile is the shortest distance between people. And when you need to reach an audience a smile will achieve that goal.

"When you think of how often I have toured and that people keep coming back to see me," he said laughingly, "it pleases me to know that they continue to show such good taste."

...ANECDOTE

Years ago when Julie Andrews was starring in an NBC variety series, one of her regular supporting players was Rich Little. One afternoon she kindly invited us to join her for afternoon tea. I was so pleased to be in her company that I'm afraid I lost my composure. When she asked me how I would like my tea, I actually said, 'hot.' The kettle had been bubbling away for several minutes.

On the "Stardust" trail with Hoagy Carmichael, 1948, for a Decca record promotion tour. He was one of my earliest interviews and a guest on the *Club Crosby* radio show.

THAT SONG OF SONGS—"STARDUST"

In 1929 a young New York lyric writer, Mitchell Parish, met an equally promising young composer from Indiana, Hoagy Carmichael, who had written an exquisite melody two years earlier. Parish was captivated by the infectious tune and was inspired to write what may be the most poetic words ever committed to a popular song. He revealed in his lyrics his fascination and obsession with the Carmichael refrain with the beautiful line, "that melody haunts my reverie."

Their collaboration is considered by musicologists as the most perfect blend of words and music—Hoagy Carmichael's eternal melody and Mitchell Parish's matchless lyrics gave the world that song of songs, "Stardust."

My interviews with the legendary songwriters Carmichael and Parish were years apart. I spent a delightful day with Mr. Carmichael during my early radio days in Toronto in 1948, and visited the memory-laden Manhattan apartment of Mr. Parish in 1983, the year following the death of his old friend and collaborator.

"We first met when we were 18 or 19 years old," Parish told me. "I was with the Mills Publishing Company at that time, making about $12 a week as a special material writer. I met Hoagy at the office one day and we became friends through our mutual love of music."

Hoagland Howard Carmichael was born November 22, 1899, in Bloomington, Indiana. His mother helped support her family by playing the piano at various functions around town. When he was a little boy she would make him an improvised bed out of two collapsible chairs, while she played with a dance band. During his formative years he became a self-taught accomplished pianist, influenced greatly by a local jazz artist, Reggie Duval, and by his mother's versatile accompaniment to silent films at their neighborhood theater. Despite his love of music he opted for a more secure future by seeking a formal education at the University of Indiana, where he graduated with a law degree.

However, as a freshman he was in great demand at campus dances, and also played piano with jazz bands around town that featured two giants of jazz, Bix Beiderbeck and Red Nichols.

It was 1927 when the first few notes of "Stardust" flitted through young Hoagie's melodic mind. A classmate, Stuart Gorrell, gave the song its title when he observed that "it sounded like dust from stars drifting down through the summer sky."

"Well, I got the idea," Carmichael revealed, "while walking across the campus one night. I had just left the college hangout called The Book Nook, and I started whistling, and from out of nowhere whistled the opening strain of 'Stardust' and I knew I had something strange and very different. That's what makes a songwriter—if you know you've written something worthwhile, then you are a songwriter; otherwise you are wasting your time."

The most romantic melody ever written was first performed by the young composer as a jazzy "stomp" number. Strange as it may seem, it enjoyed early popularity as an up-tempo dance tune by Isham Jones. Years later Artie Shaw brought it to big band prominence with his dreamy interpretation which finally placed it at the top of the hit parade. Memorable vocal versions followed by Bing Crosby, Frank Sinatra and Nat Cole. It has been estimated that it has been recorded over a thousand times.

Mitchell Parish, who was born July 10, 1900, in Shreveport, Louisiana, believed that a song's ability to survive is often determined by its early popularity: "When a song becomes an overnight hit and is overexposed, it usually kills its potential for longevity. 'Stardust' was a slow starter, winning early acceptance as a swing tune, then as a romantic ballad; it grew gradually over the years as a great standard.

"The song is unorthodox in its construction. It rambles in a way that made it impossible to imitate. There is a certain indefinable quality to it that defies analysis."

In the 1920s and 1930s, the verse of a ballad was almost as important to its acceptance by the public as the chorus. Today you rarely hear the verse to a popular song. "Stardust" is a notable exception. Its verse stands alone as a beautiful ballad, as was dramatically demonstrated by an unusual Sinatra recording of the verse alone.

The credits of the two men who gave us "Stardust" read like a litany of popular music. Carmichael's melodies included: "Up a Lazy River," "Georgia on My Mind," "Heart and Soul," "Two Sleepy People," "Old Buttermilk Sky" and the Oscar winner "In the Cool, Cool, Cool of the Evening." The Parish lyrical credits included "Deep Purple," "Moonlight Serenade," "Sweet Lorraine," "Sophisticated Lady" and "Hands Across the Table."

Hoagy Carmichael's "Stardust" trail to fame and fortune almost ended that memorable night on the campus of his alma mater as he first whistled and hummed his everlasting refrain.

"I knew I was prone to forget things," he often confessed, "so I ran back to The Book Nook to play the melody on their piano and put the notes and chords on paper. When I got home I worked on the melody, finished the chorus and some time later wrote the music for the verse.

"A few months went by, when a close university friend of mine was visiting my home in Indianapolis. One evening he asked me to play the tune I had written several months before, and when I couldn't remember it he wasn't surprised at my memory lapse. He went over to the piano and with one finger picked out the first few notes of my melody.

"Would you believe that I had almost forgotten 'Stardust' in that six- to seven-week period, and if he hadn't played it on my piano I might never have continued with the song!"

...ANECDOTE

The children of Bing Crosby's second family inherited different aspects of his talent. Harry is an accomplished guitarist, Mary a versatile actress and Nathaniel a competitive golfer. In one of the last letters I received from Bing he wrote with a touch of humor: "Kathryn and Mary are back east in a play, Nathaniel is holding down the golf course and Harry and I are singing for our supper, rehearsing a few songs to take on the road."

Anne Murray between shows in Las Vegas, 1980. A great singer and a great lady. (Photo by Elaine Atkinson)

ANNE MURRAY, CANADA'S FIRST LADY OF SONG

Anne Murray is one of the entertainment world's most versatile and enduring recording artists. Her rich, velvety contralto has captivated international audiences for over 25 years. Her appeal is universal and her repertoire is almost boundless.

"When I started I was inspired by many musical influences," she once told me. "I went right from popular songs by Perry Como, Rosemary Clooney and Bing Crosby to jazz, rock 'n' roll and folk music. I've been exposed to many musical styles. It was difficult in the beginning for people to categorize my singing. I remember one year in the early 1970s, when the nomination committee of the Grammy Awards didn't know what category to place me in, and finally settled on country and western. I probably wouldn't have won in the pop category that year. Strangely enough, my biggest country songs didn't sound like country songs to me."

The husky quality of her voice seems ideally suited to standard ballads, and it has long been my contention that she would have been as big a star in the 1930s or 1940s as she is today. In one of our earlier conversations, during a break between her shows in Las Vegas, I made that observation to her. "A lot of people have told me that my voice is suited to those old songs," she replied. "But there was a technique of singing then that has gone by the boards these days. You really have to take extensive singing lessons to do it properly."

Thinking back to the era of "the blues" and remembering the vocalists who were the outstanding exponents of that traditional musical expression, you can hear a distinct blues quality in her voice. "I've had a lot of people suggest to me that I should sing more blues; I love some of those great old blues songs, but of course we're into the pressure of getting hit records. But every now and then I can put a standard on an album. However, so many of the people who sang the blues and sang them so well were sad and down and out. I've never felt that, so I don't know if I could perform them well."

Two standards given the Murray touch on her earlier LPs are particular favorites of mine and have a wonderful blues sound, "Nevertheless" and "Together." Her fascination with old songs and old times was summed up in her 1920s-sounding hit, "Everything Old Is New Again." "Well, over the years you compile a list of songs that you would like to do, but you don't have space for them on your latest collection and the list gets longer and longer as the years go by." In 1994 she corrected that situation and realized a long-held dream to record many of her favorite old songs.

Her 29th album took her back to the last decade of the golden years of Tin Pan Alley, the 1950s, and the hits of her youth. With this collection, entitled appropriately *Croonin'*, her dream came true. "I've been burning to do this project," she said after its release. "These are the songs I grew up listening to—I cut my teeth on them. The people who sing them were real idols of mine. All the time in the studio I was thinking 'I have to do such a good job on these songs because these people I admire will be listening to them.' I didn't worry about my singing ability because it was there, but I wanted Rosemary Clooney to love 'Hey There' and I wanted Doris Day to like 'Secret Love.'

"I tried to make these songs modern and my own, yet not take away from that magic that was there originally. Everyone loved doing it. Some of the musicians were too young to remember any of the songs, but it didn't matter. For me, it was an unbelievable experience, like a trip down memory lane. It's like I was born in the wrong era." *Croonin'* includes Murray revivals of Patti Page's "Allegheny Moon," Gogi Grant's "The Wayward Wind," Julie London's "Cry Me a River" and Jo Stafford's "You Belong to Me."

Of all the ladies of song, one who is a particular favorite in the Murray household is that outstanding exponent of pop and jazz, Rosemary Clooney. "Well, Rosemary Clooney has always been one of my favorites. She is a wonderful person and she has done it all. I've traveled with my two children, but how she used to take her five on the road was amazing—I don't know how she did it. I have the utmost respect for her as a person and singer. I grew up listening to her records."

She also spent her youth listening and watching Perry Como on records and TV and was thrilled the first time she appeared on his show. "He is just a wonderful person, an absolute joy to work with. He lives with his wife down in Jupiter, Florida, and is doing what he always wanted to do, fish and golf."

Born in Springhill, Nova Scotia, where the Anne Murray Centre was opened in 1989, she is the only daughter of a country physician, James Murray, and his graduate nurse wife, Marion. With her five brothers she took an active role in sports, graduating from the University of New Brunswick with a degree in physical education.

She had a brief teaching position in Prince Edward Island before embarking on a career in the entertainment business in 1966 on the Halifax CBC-TV review *Sing Along Jubilee.* It was on that well-remembered show that she met her husband, Bill Langstroth, who was a co-host and producer of the program. They were married in 1975 and she has always insisted that he and their two children, Dawn and William Jr., are the priorities in her life. Despite her international travels and acclaim, she has remained resolutely Canadian and maintains a permanent residence and office in Toronto.

In 1970 her recording of Canadian composer Gene McLelland's northern anthem, "Snowbird," made her a global star. Since that time she has become Canada's most acclaimed performer, receiving four Grammys and 26 Canadian Juno and RPM music awards. She is a Companion of the Order of Canada and has her own star on Hollywood's Walk of Fame at the intersection of Hollywood and Vine.

She has never taken her career or fans for granted and has maintained a sense of awe at being at the pinnacle of show business. "The first time I heard my voice on a record with strings, I almost cried," she admits unashamedly. "When I won the Grammy for 'You Needed Me' I was honored to be in such elite company. I was thrilled to sell out three nights at New York's Radio City Music Hall and star for the first time in Las Vegas where Frank Sinatra's marquee was shining on the other side of the street."

✪ ✪ ✪

...ANECDOTE

Travelling along the Los Angeles freeways can be intimidating and confusing—especially if you don't concentrate on where you are going. For example, there was the time when Rich Little and I followed a car with a big dog looking out the back window. We thought we were following our wives and the Little's sheep dog on our way to visit friends. By the time we realized we were following the wrong car we were hopelessly lost. It took several phone calls and a St. Bernard rescue dog to help us find our way!

"Mr. Relaxation," Perry Como on tour in 1968. The first of my interviews with one of my favorite singers. (Photo by Andrews-Hunt)

"SING TO ME, MR. C."

In 1976 RCA Records released a Perry Como album with a most appropriate title, *A Legendary Performer*. While it acknowledged his unique place in show business, the self-deprecating entertainer continued to think of himself in a more humble way. A genuinely unassuming man, he has led an exemplary life both on and off the stage. His exceptional, mellow baritone voice and his easy-going manner have made him one of the most likable and appealing entertainers of the past 50 years.

On the Atlantic coast of South Florida, he and his wife of over 60 years, Roselle, found their "blue heaven" in the idyllic community of Jupiter, where they have lived for over 25 years. Occasionally he will venture out from his relaxed lifestyle for a fund-raising event. His voice is still as smooth as velvet and he is greeted with standing ovations wherever he appears. "You scared me half to death," he tells his audiences when they rise from their seats. "I thought maybe you were leaving the theater."

Although he hasn't recorded in a long time, he has the satisfaction of knowing his last collection was well received. It was called *Today*, and included ballads like, "The Wind Beneath My Wings" and "That's What Friends Are For," which he sang beautifully. That same year (1987) he was one of the recipients of a presidential lifetime achievement award at the annual Kennedy Center honors in Washington, D.C.

With the exception of his musical mentor, Bing Crosby, no one was more closely associated with the Christmas season than TV's "Mr. C." There was an annual Como yuletide special for 30 years, which originated from various locations around the globe. However, by the mid-1980s he had become unhappy with the network scheduling of his Christmas shows and decided not to renew his contract. "I enjoyed doing them very much," he said a few years ago, "they were always well received. It's a beautiful time of the year." But he felt that the effort and money required to produce a large-scale TV special required a better time slot than he was getting. The holiday season since then has been incomplete without a "Como Christmas" and his rendering of traditional carols and familiar seasonal songs.

Born Pierino Roland Como, May 12, 1912, in Cannonsburg, Pennsylvania, one of 13 children of Italian immigrant parents, he seemed destined, like his father, to be a barber. His apprenticeship began when he was only ten years old. By the time he was a teenager he was making a living by day practising the tonsorial art and singing with local bands by night.

During the summer of 1933, while on vacation, he won a full-time job with the Freddy Carlone Band. It was the same year that he married his childhood sweetheart.

Three years later he was signed by Ted Weems and remained with his famous orchestra until 1942. Unhappy with the constant touring of the band, which took him away from his family, he embarked on a solo career. His inspiration then and through the years was his singing idol, Bing Crosby.

"There was no one else but Bing," he said during our interview. "If you didn't sound a little like Bing, or sing like Bing, it was very difficult to get a job with an orchestra. That was the sound you listened to and it was the accepted sound. So I had my collection of Crosby records and I would listen to them as often as I could and then try to get as close to him as I could, and at times I did fairly well."

After successful 1943 radio appearances, Como was signed to a recording contract by RCA Victor. His first release, "Goodbye Sue," sold well, but his next disk, an adaptation of Chopin's "Polonaise" which was re-titled "Till the End of Time," was a million seller and made him a household name. "That was the first of 15 gold records," he told me, "and the one that kept me out of the barber business for a while."

His chain of unbroken hits over the next 15 years included his classic revivals of "Temptation" and "Prisoner of Love," and new ballads and novelty numbers like "Catch a Falling Star," "Wanted" and "Don't Let the Stars Get in Your Eyes." In the early 1970s he staged an impressive return to the hit charts with two lovely ballads, "And I Love You So" and "It's Impossible."

The Como TV years ran from 1948 to 1963. During that time the format of his show expanded from a 15-minute songfest to an hour-long award-winning musical-comedy review that made its easy-going, relaxed headliner a legendary television star.

An avid golfer and fisherman, he thoroughly enjoys his life and surroundings in Florida, where his three children, Ronnie, David and Teri and their families often visit. He is a devoted husband, father, grandfather, great-grandfather and a friend to people from all walks of life.

Reflecting on his remarkable life and career he made this heartfelt observation: "I worked with the world's greatest talents and then went home to the world's greatest woman. It was, and is, a wonderful life."

"Harry Belafonte and I have a lot in common—and we are both incredibly handsome."—Bill Cosby, backstage at the National Arts Centre, Ottawa. (Photo by Paul Atkinson)

"Mr. Show Business"

Bill Cosby is an entertainment industry unto himself. He is TV's most sought-after commercial salesman, one of television's most popular performers and a stand-up comedian who has broken attendance records throughout the English-speaking world. He is also one of the most successful comedians on records and tapes, the author of best-selling light-hearted books on the subjects of fatherhood and aging and is, of course, one of the most identifiable personalities of our time.

In the 1980s *The Bill Cosby Show* topped the ratings. The up-scale comedy series concerning a doctor, his lawyer-wife and their five children was an instant hit. The weekly escapades of the Huxtable family had universal appeal. His real-life roles of devoted husband and caring father of five came right through the television screen. He met his wife, Camille, who produced his popular video cassettes, on a blind date in 1963. His Emmy-winning show was followed by *The Cosby Mysteries*, which gave him a change of pace and another popular program. In the fall of 1996 he returned to situation comedy with a weekly series that once again stressed family values and his own outlook on life.

Despite his phenomenal success he is to both co-workers and fans a friendly and uncomplicated person. On his shows, however, he is firmly in charge and exercises control over most aspects of their production.

He was most accommodating when I met with him between shows during one of his North American tours. There is a showbiz adage that warns actors not to work with children, because they are scene-stealers. Bill Cosby has contradicted that old axiom throughout his career and did so during our interview.

"Some people feel that the thunder is being stolen from them. I relinquish the thunder to the child. I've always felt that we are there to entertain and that's all that matters. I have a genuine love of children. I am also aware of a fact that very few entertainers consider, that these children will become adults and be tomorrow's co-workers and audience." Whether he is taping one of his award-winning Jell-O commercials or working on a situation comedy, he has a rapport with children that few performers could achieve. His Saturday morning cartoon series, *Fat Albert and the Cosby Kids*, was endorsed by parents and critics alike.

His racial background, his poor circumstances as a child, his struggle to achieve success and his ability to see the amusing side of life all contributed to his distinctive brand of humor. "I didn't know my style or how to write for myself early in my career. I really hadn't found out the best way to convey what I do; when I eventually found my style it became much easier. I can write for myself on the spot now, which some people call ad-libbing; I call it writing on the spot."

He was born July 12, 1938, in a Philadelphia ghetto and raised by his mother and maternal grandfather. It was in his below-par grammar school that he met the kids who were the models for his comedy characters, like Weird Old Harold and Fat Albert. ("We used to go to every horror picture in town. We would walk for miles to see Frankenstein. We had the best seats in the theater, we'd sit right up front, but we never saw the monster because we were too scared to look at him!")

A high school dropout, he continued his education at night school and went on in later years to win a bachelor's degree at Temple University. In 1972 he received a master's degree and four years later his doctorate in education.

In 1965, after becoming established on the night club circuit, Cosby won the TV role that was the turning point in his career, appearing with Robert Culp as an espionage agent in *I Spy*. He was the first black actor to win a starring role in an American television drama. However, as he told me, it was a move that was not without controversy.

"I don't take any credit for what happened. I was just standing in the right spot at the right time. I don't say this out of great humility; it's the way it was. But at that time, being from a minority, you were at the mercy of those who had the money and made the decisions whether or not you worked. Sheldon Leonard picked me from the field of actors and said, 'You're going to work on *I Spy*!' Now, to explain the situation, and how the media thought back then, they asked me if I thought the American public would accept a Negro in a series; I never brought this question up because I was too busy trying to survive as an actor. But the thinking and attitudes in America at that time were reflected in their questions. Of course, when I began working with Sheldon, Bob Culp and their associates, they helped make everything a lot more comfortable for me."

Harry Belafonte and Sidney Poitier are two of Cosby's closest friends. They were among his earliest supporters. During one of my Belafonte interviews Harry recalled their first encounter with the Cosby brand of humor: "Sidney and I first saw him at a night club here in New York called Basin Street East. We always made it our business to be supportive of new black artists. We had heard and read a lot about Bill, but when we attended his performance we knew that we were in the presence of a man who was truly gifted and brought another style to the traditional look of black humor. He humanized, not just characterized, black humor. It had always fallen into a certain linguistic pattern and went into a certain direction and here was Bill Cosby taking it to a new level and into another direction. We felt that he would make an important impact on his time and that we would make ourselves available to him, not only with our friendship, but with whatever we had to offer to be supportive. He didn't need us because he did it all on his own. We became good friends and one of the most delightful times I ever had was the film we did together, *Uptown Saturday Night*."

The easygoing Cosby's favorite Belafonte anecdote occurred during a benefit concert at the Hollywood Bowl. "Harry, Barbara Streisand, Herb Alpert and I were each given an hour for rehearsal. Streisand showed up with her entourage, Harry with his group and Alpert with his band. Streisand rehearsed with a string section, Harry went on stage with backup singers and dancers, and Alpert put his musicians through their paces. Then the director called out, 'Okay, the Cosby rehearsal now!' I walked out with my microphone in my back pocket, stuck it into a plug, put the mike in my mouth and made a few strange noises and told the director that everything was fine for me. From the other side of the stage Harry in disbelief yelled out, 'What! That's it! And you do this for a living?' We have such fun together—-I'm so glad that I know him and that he is my good friend."

✪ ✪ ✪

...ANECDOTE

The Cosby comedic style was never more in evidence than the night we met for the first time. My son Paul accompanied me to his dressing room and when I told him that Paul was one of his biggest fans, he jumped from his chair, looked me in the eye and said, "He's a big fan of mine—and you never told me!"

Harry Belafonte—an early interview (our first meeting), 1960.

A Matchless Entertainer

Harry Belafonte, a matchless entertainer and universal man, has captivated audiences for over 40 years with his dynamic performances and his songs of joy, anguish and social concern. In recent years he has devoted much of his time as a goodwill ambassador for the United Nations. With his wife, Julie, he has traveled extensively, visiting the children of developing countries. He is a passionate spokesman on their behalf.

Along with Peter Ustinov, Liv Ullman and the late Audrey Hepburn, Harry has continued the UNICEF mission of its first spokesperson, Danny Kaye. He was appointed Goodwill Ambassador following the death of the famous comedian in 1987. During our last interview at his New York office, he recalled Kaye's outstanding commitment to the children of the world:

Harry Belafonte

"From the arts community it is proper to say that he was the founder of UNICEF. His incredible talent was put into the service of that organization when it needed to have visibility in order for people to understand the meaning of UNICEF. When he became its roving ambassador, he traveled the world seeking commitments from heads of state of different ideologies to protect and nurture children. The humanitarian work of the UN would not be known to many people if artists had not become involved and used their platforms to speak on its behalf."

As an entertainer who is greatly respected by his colleagues, Harry has had a dramatic impact, through his recordings, films and concerts, on both popular and folk music. His impressive repertoire ranges all the way from "Island in the Sun," "Mary's Boy Child," "Abraham, Martin and John," and "Try to Remember," to "Matilda" and "The Banana Boat Song." In his individualistic style and manner he reflects like no one else the traditions and concerns of people and places that share our global village.

Born in New York City March 1, 1927, of Jamaican parents, he spent several years as a boy in Jamaica absorbing and growing in the life and customs of that beautiful island. His 1955 album *Calypso* made him an international star and popularized the infectious music of the Caribbean around the world.

"Many of the songs I sing," he recalled, "had their roots in traditional folk material out of the West Indies, and in the hands of skillful poets they were developed into ballads that gave audiences an easier link to the subject matter and to the islands. In simplifying this material I hoped that people around the world would be carried a little further in appreciating the content and rhythms. Given the popularity of calypso and reggae today I like to think my early recordings acquainted audiences with the dialects and patois of the Caribbean. One of those songs, however, 'Jamaica Farewell,' had instant universal appeal because of its beautiful melody and feelings of nostalgia and belonging that we all share."

The friendship that began over 35 years ago between Harry and me often has us exchanging anecdotes about our families whenever we meet. He has three daughters, Adrienne, Gina and Shari (the latter a successful model and actress), and a son, David, who is the stage sound engineer for his famous father's concerts.

A Belafonte performance is always an entertaining blend of music, comedy and social awareness. Although he still accepts occasional bookings, he is finding more time these days for special projects and charitable works. A personal friend of Dr. Martin Luther King (he was one of the executors of his estate) and both John and Robert Kennedy, he has received humanitarian and artistic honors from around the world, including Washington's prestigious Kennedy Honor.

He was also the first recipient of the National American Film Foundation's Arts and Justice Award. This New York-based organization gives financial support to movies supporting social issues. His pals Bill Cosby and Sidney Poitier were the co-emcees of the presentation. During my conversation with Cosby he expressed high praise of Harry as both a friend and a performer:

"I don't think anyone can match in taste and class Harry Belafonte. Anyone can spend thousands of dollars on costuming, musicians and the best songs, but class you cannot buy. Harry Belafonte has class! He meticulously puts together for each minute of every show, pound for pound with no fat, the most professional program possible. Belafonte is that well-rounded and highly intelligent a performer. Harry was also one of the first entertainers to really step out and say what was on his mind and in his heart and publicly combat racism and injustice."

Belafonte the World Citizen has never avoided controversy for the sake of popularity. He has been an eloquent and effective spokesman for causes that have touched the conscience and soul of humanity.

"So many of the causes that I found myself involved with years ago were not popular. Back then, many people in America really didn't want to hear about civil rights or be concerned about the complaints and the protests of so many millions of people who were ground under. Those who sought to be one of their spokespersons or who took up with Dr. King were looked upon as provocateurs, spoilers or misfits. It was very difficult then to say, there is something here that is truly dishonorable that we have a moral responsibility to change and even if you denounce me I have no choice but to stay the course! It did finally grip not only the U.S. but the whole world, and we did get civil rights and the human family had a greater sense of nobility."

A World War II navy veteran, he was opposed to the war in Vietnam, and was active in the peace movement during those turbulent years. "Many of us in the entertainment business felt we had no business there, and if we did have some commitment there it should have been on an infinitely more humane and different level. Consequently some people considered us very unpatriotic. If anything I am more committed to the American Constitution than those who were doing things that were not constitutional. I have felt a deep obligation to speak on behalf of world peace, the anti-nuclear movement and world hunger. I have had a very rewarding life, because all my concerns have come to pass, and I like to think I was on the right side of it all."

Harry Belafonte—an animated conversation (no doubt we were laughing at the antics of Bill Cosby), 1980.

"A charming and gracious hostess"—with Dinah Shore at her home in Beverly Hills—1984. (Photo by Elaine Atkinson)

The Songbird of the South

Dinah Shore's charming and gracious manner captivated television audiences for over four decades. Her engaging personality made her one of the most successful performers of her time. She was so closely associated with her roles of variety and talk show hostess that even people of her era sometimes forget that she was one of the great song stylists of the 20th century. A genuinely warm and thoughtful person, her death in 1994 was mourned by people from all walks of life who knew and loved her.

On a beautiful, sunny California day in February 1984, my wife and I were guests at her charming Beverly Hills home, which was adjacent to the Beverly Hills Hotel. We met in her comfortable, airy living-room, which overlooked the tennis court. A year later we met again and renewed our friendship.

Dinah Shore

From the time she was a little girl she loved to sing. "I thought that everybody sang," was the way she remembered her childhood. "I couldn't understand as I grew older why everybody was excited about my singing. Almost everyone I knew in Tennessee liked to sing. My mother was a wonderful singer with a pretty mezzo soprano voice and my father had a lovely tenor voice. However, my older sister Bessie couldn't carry a tune—but she did play the piano. I was the show-off from the time I was three or four, getting up and singing anywhere or any time. When I went to New York I was told that there was something unusual in the way I sang, which amazed me. I went there to be an actress but everywhere I went they wanted me to sing. When I would audition for acting parts I would get nervous and my accent would become more pronounced and they weren't writing too many roles then for southerners. I got into singing out of necessity."

Born March 1, 1917, in Winchester, Tennessee, but raised in neighboring Nashville, she began life as Frances Rose Shore. Her father, Solomon, was from a family of European teachers, and emigrated to the United States where he was a self-employed businessman. Her mother, Anna, who died while she was in her teen years, was a music aficionado and sports enthusiast. In high school Dinah was active in theatrical productions and was a football cheerleader, which put a strain on her voice and ended her formal vocal lessons. While still in her teens she was introduced to radio on two Nashville stations. She attended Vanderbilt University and graduated with a Bachelor of Arts degree in sociology.

It was Martin Block of WNEW, New York, the first of the famous radio disk jockeys, who was responsible for her name change. Answering an "audition call" while on a brief visit to Manhattan, the young Miss Shore chose the southern hit "Dinah" for her performance. Block was very impressed with her rendition of the song. "He couldn't remember my name," she recalled. "There were several of us auditioning. I was on my way home to Nashville from summer camp. We had all performed and were sitting around when he said, 'Dinah, I'd like to hear you sing one more time.' Everybody looked around wondering who he was talking to and when no one answered I realized he meant me, and I said excitedly, 'Oh, yes! Of course!' And that was my name forever after."

Early in her radio career she had an unexpected guest during a program rehearsal, the great composer of "the blues," W.C. Handy. When he heard Dinah's rendition of a song he had written in 1912, with tears in his eyes he said, "My dear, 'Memphis Blues' was never really sung before. You turned the clock back 30 years for me."

Her southern roots and love of "the blues" won her a spot early in her career on the well-remembered network radio show, *The Chamber Music Society of Lower Basin Street.* "I worked on that program on Sunday afternoons while I was still singing on WNEW. One of Eddie Cantor's daughters was a regular listener and she brought me to his attention." In 1942, Cantor was at the height of his popularity on radio and in movies. The famous musical-comedy star was so impressed with her singing that he signed her to a contract. She remembered their meeting with gratitude and affection:

"There are certain milestones in your career and Eddie Cantor was definitely the turning point for me. I made my father a promise that if I went to the big wolfish city I would not be a band singer, so Eddie relieved me of that choice when he selected me for his radio show. There is a lovely story about him that I like to recall. When I went to audition for him I arrived at the studio terrified; my knees were knocking, my heart was quaking and my mouth was bone dry. I began singing, but I couldn't see anyone in the control room and assumed they were in another room. I continued singing but no one said anything and I began to think they had gone home, when a voice on the speaker said, 'Could we hear some more please.' About 45 minutes later this lovely, spare, kindly man came out of the booth and held out his hand to me—it was Eddie Cantor! He kissed me on the cheek and said, 'You will forgive me for keeping you singing so long, but I figured it's the last time I will ever hear you for nothing.' Which meant I had the job. I was on his program for three years.

"He also bought the rights to my first hit song, 'Yes, My Darling Daughter.' It was recorded on a Monday, I did his show on Wednesday and by Friday it was a best-seller. When he moved his program to Hollywood I appeared with him in my first film, *Thank Your Lucky Stars*, which featured an all-star cast."

As a young child Dinah was stricken with polio, but through her own determined efforts and her parents' strong support she made a full recovery. Her family and friends believed that her physical therapy led to her love of sports.

"It was Eddie Cantor who started the March of Dimes," she recalled. "It was his concept and it was enthusiastically supported by President Roosevelt. He campaigned vigorously on its behalf, telling people that if they would send ten cents to the President they could start a 'March of Dimes' and help find a cure for polio."

In 1943 she met and married actor George Montgomery, who was under contract to 20th Century Fox before he began his military service. Although they parted 18 years later they remained good friends. He and their two children, Melisa Ann and John David, were by her side when she died of cancer, just a few days short of her 77th birthday.

Despite her age her death was a shock to her friends and fans. When she was well into her seventh decade she continued to lead a healthy and active life style. Her youthful appearance belied her years. She was proud of her annual golf and tennis tournaments, which played important roles in advancing the stature of women's sports. She also loved cooking and promoted nutritious meals with her two popular books, *Someone's in the Kitchen with Dinah* and *The Dinah Shore Cookbook.*

During the war years she was a "Sweetheart of the Armed Forces," tirelessly working on behalf of the war effort at fund-raising rallies, at camp shows and on the air. She toured overseas, when the issue was still in doubt in Europe, singing for the troops while sniper fire and falling bombs on more than one occasion disrupted her show. It was an emotional experience that she treasured throughout her life:

"It was a privilege to perform for people who really needed you—servicemen whose brief respites you tried to make a little more pleasant. I've always felt a great satisfaction in being able to deliver music and I will never get over the joy of being there at a time that was important. Whether it was for a group of 25 or 5000 for whom you were allowed to sing, they were moments that nothing can touch. I had been married only a short time when the tours began and being away from my husband was the hardest part of all, because he was in the army too."

At that point in our reminiscing I said to her that I would never again hear the song "I'll Walk Alone" without thinking of her. "There were some wonderful songs back then," she replied. "'I'll Be Seeing You,' 'I Don't Want to Walk without You,' and some of the blues ballads like 'Blues in the Night' came out about that time."

It was Dinah's radio experience that prepared her for a career move to television. *The Dinah Shore Show*, which ran for 10 years beginning in 1951, established her as one of the most successful entertainers in TV history. It was followed by her talk shows which ran in four different formats until only a short time before her death. She was the recipient of more TV awards (including 10 Emmys) than any other performer. "I guess television is where I found my niche. I love to appear in public and we did those shows before an audience." Her singing commercial "See the U.S.A. in a Chevrolet" was as well known as many hit songs. She accidentally developed her trademark sign-off, blowing a kiss to her audience, when she was padding for time on a show that was running short.

In the formative years of her career the trade papers capitalized on her southern accent and upbringing, with predictable captions for their rave reviews, like "The Songbird of the South" and "The Nashville Nightingale." During the 1940s and 1950s nine of her recordings sold over one million copies and three topped the two million mark. Her biggest hit record, "Buttons and Bows," was a novelty song that was introduced by Bob Hope in one of his films, the western spoof *The Paleface*.

"That record only runs a minute and 45 seconds," she reminded me. "The stop watch broke that night and we thought it was about a minute longer. The disk jockeys wouldn't play records that were too long, but that one was really short. It was a big, big seller. But we recorded other songs several times, 'Blues in the Night,' 'The Gypsy' and 'Laughing on the Outside,' and it's hard to know which of the versions sold the most."

On March 15, 1982, at the Songwriters' Hall of Fame dinner, Dinah Shore received the prestigious Lifetime Achievement Award. That evening the recipient of the Johnny Mercer Award, named after the founder of the Songwriters' Hall of Fame, was another towering figure of popular music, composer Harold Arlen. I had the great privilege that night of being a guest of the president of the National Academy of Popular Music, Sammy Cahn, for the ceremonies at the New York Hilton Hotel. Harold Arlen was one of the most influential writers in Dinah's career, and most appropriately she presented a special musical salute to him with an outstanding medley of his memorable songs. The reaction of that dinner audience of show business luminaries was electrifying. She received a standing ovation. Since she was surrounded by her contemporaries following her performance, I felt I should resist the temptation to elbow my way through the crowd to offer my congratulations.

"I wish you hadn't resisted the temptation," was her gracious response, when I told her how deeply I was moved that evening. "There is a very special quality about Harold Arlen," she continued, "he was writing blues songs long before anyone else in the pop field. He was the one who took the blues and gave it a pop form. When I made the Goldwyn picture with Danny Kaye, *Up In Arms*, they had Harold Arlen and Ted Koeler write two of my songs, 'Now I Know' and 'Tess's Torch Song.' I guess I've sung more Harold Arlen ballads in my lifetime than the songs of any other composer. The medley that night was my way of showing my deep appreciation to him. I'm so glad you enjoyed it—that meant a lot to me. I loved that evening."

It can be stated unequivocally that Dinah Shore, both on and off stage, was universally loved. The former president of 20th Century Fox, Marvin Davis, summed up her impact on the entertainment world when he said in a statement following her death: "We have lost one of the voices that defined an era."

"Working hard on his golf game and getting laughs." My favorite photo with the one and only Bob Hope.

"Thanks for the Memories"

Bob Hope, the master showman who elevated the comedy monologue to an entertainment art form, honed and refined his distinctive brand of humor during the wartime years of the 1940s. His irreverent and breezy style of delivery never failed to amuse and delight the men and women of the Allied forces. As the entertainment world's most famous "soldier in greasepaint" he has brought laughter and a touch of home to service personnel around the globe—from World War II to Desert Storm.

I first met the legendary showman in 1949 and have had the privilege of interviewing him several times over the years. We last met at his beautiful estate in Toluca Lake, California, where he and his wife Dolores and their four adopted children took up residence in 1950.

There are two stately houses on their property. Upon entering the first building, accompanied by his long-time agent Frank Reo, I was surprised to discover that it was an office complex. I was told that it was the original Hope residence but became the headquarters of his enterprises. One room contains copies of all his movies, radio and television programs, and broadcast scripts. The walls are adorned with photos of him and Bing Crosby. As we left the office building through a rear door we walked across a courtyard passing Mrs. Hope, who gave us a friendly welcome—we were on our way to the second building which is the family dwelling. It is not only a sumptuous house but a warm and inviting home. My interview took place in the sunroom overlooking his private 9-hole golf course.

His humor has always been topical, which he believes is one of the reasons he has endured. When he was on tour an advance man would travel ahead to soak up local atmosphere. "When you talk about current events and names in the news an audience anticipates a punch line; you nudge them with a topic and that's when you get laughs and results." So said the master of the one-liner as we began our conversation. When I asked him if he had any advice for young comedians, he responded in typical fashion: "I suggest they get out of the business, it's rough and we don't need them. No, I'm kidding; there's lots of opportunities for young people on local TV shows and in clubs. If you have talent and persevere they'll put you on. Usually any kind of talent is recognized."

It was over 55 years ago that the ageless performer made his military showbiz debut. He remembers the circumstances that led to that event vividly: "In 1941 I was doing my radio show for Pepsodent at the NBC studios in Hollywood. Following one of our broadcasts I received an invitation to visit March Field Air Force Base; I thought it might be a good opportunity to try out a few service gags. So a week later I was on a bus with my radio gang heading for Riverside, California, where the base was located. Well, we did our variety show for these Air Force guys and they were a sensational audience.

"The following year we did our first tour of military centers and traveled as far as Alaska. In 1943 we went overseas for the first time to Britain and North Africa; we toured the South Pacific in '44 and then returned to England and Africa in '45. From there we went on to the

Italian front and following D-Day visited the front lines and hospitals from Normandy to Paris and on into Germany. In between our overseas tours we did shows at sea, at bases in the Caribbean and at camps all over the U.S. and Canada."

Throughout the dark days of the 1940s Hope and his pal Bing Crosby were not only the two biggest stars in the entertainment world, but the top comedy team in show business, with their zany "Road" movies, radio shows and tireless touring for the war effort. "We had a lot of respect for one another," Bob said affectionately. "As you know he had a great sense of humor and we had a lot of fun and traveled extensively together. I guess we played at least a hundred exhibition games of golf for charities around the world."

During one of my interviews with Bing, he recalled their first encounter: "I first met Bob at the Capitol Theater in New York where we were on the same bill. He was doing an act with a girl who played straight for him and he was a wisecracking comedian. I was just starting out as one of the Rhythm Boys and we used to go together to the Friar's Club where all the actors hung out. I saw a lot of Bob in those days and we have been great friends ever since."

Four years later they were reunited at the Capitol Theater. "We were back in New York in 1932," Bob recalled. "I was the emcee and Bing was the headliner—he was a radio and recording star by that time. We were there for two weeks doing four shows a day. By the second week we started ad-libbing and we worked up an impromptu act. Five years later I was signed by Paramount and moved to California. Bing was already a big star. A short time after my arrival I went down to Del Mar Race Track where Bing was one of the owners, and at his invitation attended one of their Saturday night parties. We got up and did the same act we did at the Capitol Theater and a couple of guys from Paramount who were there thought we really worked well together. They thought we were ad-libbing and said, 'We've got to get a script for them,' so they got a story called 'Flight to Singapore' and changed the title to *Road to Singapore*. That was 1939 and that's how the 'Roads' started. We made seven of them."

On their way to Zanzibar, Morocco, Utopia, Rio, Bali and Hong Kong, there was as much comedy on the sets as there was on the screen. "We did a lot of ad-libbing," Bob admitted. "The great writers of the pictures, Hartman and Butler, who did a wonderful job preparing the scripts, used to walk on the set and we would say, 'If you hear one of your lines yell Bingo!' Bing and I would add our own material and once in a while lose some of their lines, but the wonderful construction they did for those pictures always came through."

The make-believe rivalry between Bob and Bing emphasized their imaginary deficiencies and questionable attributes and gave Crosby many quotable one-liners about Hope's vocalizing. In reality Bob has a very pleasant voice that he says he inherited from his mother. Before he turned to comedy he was a song and dance man, and later as a Broadway star introduced great standard ballads on the musical stage. "I've been singing ever since I started in show business," he reminded me. "On Broadway I introduced 'I Can't Get Started with You' in the *Ziegfield Follies* of 1935, 'It's Delovely' with Ethel Merman in 1936 in Cole Porter's *Red, Hot and Blue*, and 'Smoke Gets in Your Eyes' by Jerome Kern back in '33 in *Roberta*. But when I got to Paramount, there was so much jealousy from that older actor, Crosby! In truth, Bing and I did a lot of numbers together and he was a delight to work with."

Apart from the 'Road' pictures, Hope's box office hits have included *The Cat and the Canary*, *The Ghost Breakers*, *The Paleface*, *The Seven Little Foys* and *Beau James*, to name only a few.

One of the world's most identifiable American performers was born in England. His mother was the daughter of a Welsh sea captain and his father was a stonemason by trade. He was a little boy when his family emigrated to the U.S., where his father had relatives in Cleveland, Ohio. He was christened Leslie Townes Hope; his second name was for his mother's side of the family. Early in his career he decided to drop Leslie and call himself "Bob," which seemed more appropriate for a vaudevillian. He was one of seven sons, and coincidentally, Bing also came from a family of seven, two girls and five boys.

It is a staggering fact that the Hope clan celebrated his 93rd birthday May 29, 1996. Sadly, at this writing his failing health has forced him to give up touring and performing. But, as he reminded me during our last interview in 1985, longevity runs in his family. His grandfather Hope was almost a centenarian.

"Dolores and I went over to England for the first time in 1939, when my grandfather was still alive; he was 96 at the time. I invited all my relatives to a local pub in Eltham, where I was born, and about 40 of them showed up. I got up and welcomed everyone, told a few jokes and told them how great it was to be there, and then just making conversation I said I understood my Uncle Tom was a wonderful whistler. My grandfather interrupted me and said, 'Sit down boy! You don't know these people very well; it's Uncle Frank who whistles; I'll take over.' He proceeded to introduce all my relations, told a few funny family stories and did a little dance. It was quite an evening and he was just amazing.

"Four years later I was in Warton doing a big show for the air force when my manager informed me that my grandfather was out in the audience. I was quite surprised that he was still active. I introduced him and he walked up the aisle supported only by his cane. I helped him up on the stage and he joked with me and gave a warm little speech. He wished everyone good luck on their missions and offered them his prayers. Two weeks later I was in Birmingham when I was notified that he had passed away, just one month short of his 100th birthday. He was a wonderful old gentleman."

During his first visit to England the unflappable Mr. Hope had an awkward but amusing experience. While in Eltham arrangements were made for him to visit the row house where he thought he was born. "I knocked on the door," he recalled with a chuckle, "and the couple living there greeted me with blank stares. I told them who I was and the purpose of my visit, but they were not impressed and didn't invite me in for a look at the place. So I left somewhat embarrassed, only to discover later that it was the wrong house. Then years later on a trip back to my home town for the dedication of a theater named after me I finally got to visit the house where I really was born. The folks living there were most hospitable; however, they were not amused when I made a joke on a BBC-TV special that 'my house was bombed during the war—by the British!' But we made up and they invited me back to the house for tea."

Spanning five decades, the Hope memory bank is filled to capacity with names of people and places from the war years that he has never forgotten. "We had the most exciting shows," he recalled fondly, "with Hollywood's top stars and our own wonderful regulars, Frances Langford, Jerry Colonna and the bands of Skinnay Ennis and Les Brown. Each show was an emotional experience."

While some of his wartime shows and personal encounters may be hard for him to recall, they are still fond memories for the men and women he entertained. He still corresponds with veterans who found special meaning in the title of his theme song, "Thanks for the Memory," and who cherish a memorable moment they had with him. He remembers them with great affection: "They were all grateful for the time we spent with them and we were very grateful for what they had done for all of us—laying their lives on the line for our freedom."

It was in a star-studded movie musical, *The Big Broadcast of 1938*, that Bob first featured his theme song in a duet with Shirley Ross. Since he has consistently performed parodies of the Leo Robin-Ralph Rainger ballad, I wondered if there had been an occasion when he couldn't remember the original lyrics. "Let me tell you that I would have trouble remembering even one chorus," was his reply. "Leo Robin wrote four or five original choruses and after he passed away his widow sent me all the special lyrics he had written over the years, and I was amazed at his output. On account of doing a different version of the song every week on radio and later on TV, I would have trouble remembering the original lyrics. Shirley Ross and I did another ballad that was a movie standout called 'Two Sleepy People,' written by Frank Loesser and Hoagy Carmichael."

In 1933 he was appearing in the Jerome Kern musical *Roberta* on Broadway. Actor George Murphy was also in the cast and it was their first hit show. It was at that time that Bob met Dolores Reid, who became his wife a year later—it's a charming romantic story:

"George Murphy and I went to the Lamb's Club one night for a beer. He asked me if I would like to hear a pretty girl sing, and we went over to the Vogue Club and Dolores was singing 'Paper Moon' and several great tunes and I said to George, 'How long has this been going on?' I met her after her performance and asked her to please come and see me in *Roberta*. She thought I was a chorus boy or had some minor role, and when she saw me doing this big part she was so embarrassed that she didn't come back to see me after the show. So I went back to see her and we sat outside the Delmonico Hotel where she was staying, but I never got inside the hotel. Then she went to Florida and it bothered me that I couldn't see more of her; I kept calling her and I fell into that trap and that was 51 years ago." Then, after a slight pause, with a twinkle in his eyes, he added, "I tell you I should never have gone to that Vogue Club." In 1996 they celebrated their 64th wedding anniversary.

Despite his years of international acclaim he continues to see himself in simple terms and as an uncomplicated person. We all have a public image of Bob Hope, but I wondered what image he has of himself. "That's a wonderful question," he responded, "I'll have to think about that. It may take a couple of days. But, put simply, my own image of myself is a fella working on his golf game and working hard to get laughs." He has succeeded in doing just that and has kept the world laughing for over 60 years.

✪ ✪ ✪

With Bob Hope and Rich Little at the Hope estate, Toluca Lake, CA (Bob was amazed at Rich's impressions), March 1985.

[*Editor's note: Gord Atkinson's radio series* The Life and Times of Bob Hope *was the winner of a 1986 Gabriel Award from the American National Catholic Association of Broadcasters.*]

With Bing in 1965—prior to a TV special.

The Crosby Years

Bing Crosby was the most popular entertainer of his time and had perhaps a greater impact on show business than any other performer of the 20th century. MCA Records, who own all his Brunswick/Decca records that were produced between 1931 and 1957, back up that statement with staggering figures.

Twenty-five years ago the international sale of just his Decca records was said to be in excess of 400 million copies. During a 1993 MCA video tribute to Bing ("His Legendary Years"), hosted by actor-comedian Dennis Miller, it was estimated that a billion Crosby records have been sold throughout the world! Forty of his records were number one hits and twenty-one sold more than a million copies. Three hundred and forty of his disks made the hit charts. Fourteen of the songs he introduced in his movies were nominated for the Oscar and four won

Academy Awards: "Sweet Leilani," "White Christmas," "Swinging On A Star" and "In the Cool, Cool, Cool of the Evening."

As an actor he starred in 29 top-grossing films and was the only star to be number one at the box office for five consecutive years. He received Academy Award nominations for *The Country Girl* and *The Bells of St. Mary's* and won the best-actor Oscar in *Going My Way.* He and Bob Hope were one of the screen's most popular comedy teams. His radio show was the top variety program of its era and his television specials were always high in the ratings.

Bob Hope put it all into perspective when he made this comment to me about the Crosby legacy: "The marvellous thing about Bing is that we still have his wonderful recordings and films and they keep putting them on, especially during the Christmas season—and they are permanent. They will be here when we are gone and that's a comforting thought."

It was my privilege to produce an authorized 14-hour radio documentary on Bing's life and career, *The Crosby Years*, for his 50th year in show business. I was fortunate to talk to over 50 of his friends and co-stars, and conduct lengthy interviews with him at his suburban San Francisco estate. The series also inspired a book entitled *A Voice For All Seasons*, on which I collaborated with my writer friend Sheldon O'Connell of Vancouver. My interviews with Bing took place in the den and library of his gracious French Provincial home in Hillsboro, California, during July and October of 1974. We were joined during the breaks in our taping by his wife Kathryn and their eldest son Harry.

The radio series was heard around the world in 1975 and re-broadcast two years later, following Bing's sudden death from a heart attack on a golf course in Spain October 14, 1977. He had just completed an engagement at London's Palladium Theatre and flew to Spain for a short vacation.

He was born May 3, 1903 in Tacoma, Washington, but raised in neighboring Spokane. Harry Lillis Crosby got his nickname from a newspaper comic strip. "Yes, the comic strip is where I got the name originally," he told me. "There was a comic strip called the 'Bingville Bugle' and in the strip was a character named Bingo and when I was three or four years old I used to go around saying 'Bingo, Bingo,' and that was reduced to Bing and that was the name that was hung on me."

In the course of our taped conversations there were fascinating insights into his movie and recording careers. He looked back on the production of films during Hollywood's golden years with mixed emotions: "My chief recollections of movie making in the 1930s was the trouble they used to have with sound—recording songs or photographing a song. Just to do one chorus used to take two or three days, because of the problems they had in placing the microphones to pick up the voice, without having the orchestra overpower the vocalist. But it was a lot of fun in those days. Picture making was more leisurely, the schedules were not quite so demanding, the budgets were a little more elastic and there was more socializing and more good times. For instance, back then at Paramount there was Marlene Dietrich, Gary Cooper, Frederick March, Fred MacMurray, Bob [Hope] of course, and any number of picture people along dressing room row. It was a great place to visit, play cards or carry on with one thing or another, it was quite a social atmosphere.

"The most satisfying movies to me were the 'Road' pictures. I believe they provided people with a lot of fun. They were a lot of laughs to make with Bob and Dorothy Lamour; Jerry Colonna was in a couple of them, and we always had some interesting and amusing people in these pictures. *Going My Way* gave me the most gratification because it had an eminent success. It's still playing on television, entertaining people."

The man who was most responsible for Bing's musical versatility and amazing body of work was the late record producer Jack Kapp. "He was indeed my Svengali as far as the record business was concerned; he started out with the idea of broadening my musical horizons. Jack got me into every kind of musical category, western, Irish, Hawaiian, Latin American, Christmas songs and carols, singing with groups, singing with jazz bands, Dixieland bands, symphony orchestras, with practically every kind of a vocal and musical combination you could think of and almost every kind of song. For instance, it was his idea that I get into the Victor Herbert category." In 50 years of recording the Crosby library had over 2000 commercial releases. Rosemary Clooney described it as "a monumental body of work."

Since Bing never took his work or himself too seriously, it was a revelation when he told me that he was pleased with a few of his recorded performances. "There were a couple of records that I always thought sounded pretty good. One was called *Isle of Golden Dreams.* I did a few of the Richard Tauber things like 'Yours Is My Heart Alone' and some of the Victor Herbert songs. I thought the voice sounded pretty good on those, but maybe it was just because I was congratulating myself on having entered into a new field."

At the radio awards in San Fransisco, September 19, 1976, with Bing and his radio announcer of 25 years, Ken Carpenter.

Occasionally someone will ask me if there is one recording in my collection of Crosbyana that is my favorite. From a performance level there are too many superb recordings by Bing to pick even a handful of personal favorites. However, I do have a sentimental favorite that I heard for the first time at his home—the story follows.

After completing *The Crosby Years*, my wife and I traveled to Hillsboro and presented the entire radio series to him. It was contained in a hand-crafted wooden case with a gold maple leaf insignia. Bing and Kathryn expected our visit but they were not aware of our planned presentation. As we arrived we were met by their butler, Alan Fisher, who by now had become a friend. We carefully took the cabinet out of its case and placed it on a table in the foyer. We could hear

Bing and Kathryn singing to piano accompaniment in another room. Alan told them of our arrival and they walked into the foyer and greeted us warmly. Bing was delighted with the tapes of the series and the handsome cabinet.

Presenting *The Crosby Years'* tapes to Bing, while Kathryn Crosby looks on. January 1976. (Photo by Elaine Atkinson)

Following a pleasant conversation and the taking of a few commemorative photographs we entered the living-room. We were then introduced to their pianist, and as we watched, they finished rehearsing for a forthcoming benefit performance. Then we were taken by surprise when Bing said: "There's a new song called 'At My Time of Life' that was written for a musical adaptation of Charles Dickens' *Great Expectations*. John Mills is appearing in it in London and it is heading for Broadway. I'm going to record it next week. It's quite a song. I'd like to hear what you think of it." As we sat on French Provincial chairs in his beautiful living-room he began to sing. The piano player was obviously ad-libbing the accompaniment. His voice was strong and mellow and filled the room. He was 72 years old and the song was most appropriate for his time of life. It was a private performance just for us and left us almost speechless.

At the conclusion of the song Bing told us that he would be in

Hollywood in a few days for a recording date and invitated us to attend. As we left the Crosby residence Kathryn suggested that his rendering of the song was his way of saying "thank you" for my radio series on his life and times. The piano player confirmed to us that he had heard the song for the first time that morning.

The following week Bing called Rich Little's home in Malibu, where we were vacationing, and invited us to lunch and the recording session. Arriving at Western Studios in Hollywood I was especially pleased that as we entered the sound booth Bing began to record "At My Time of Life." Later, at our luncheon date, we were joined by Bing's English producer and his musical director, Ken Barnes and Pete Moore. We were also joined by Sonny Burke, who had directed many sessions for Bing and Frank Sinatra. He told us, while we were waiting for Bing to join us, that the first time Crosby and Sinatra recorded together everyone wondered at what time of the day the session would take place. "Bing preferred morning dates and Frank would only record in the evening. But Sinatra bowed to his boyhood idol and was on the set bright and early."

A year later my wife and I were in Britain and at the invitation of Ken Barnes visited his London studios. Ken was responsible for revitalizing Bing's recording career and produced an amazing collection of Crosby cassettes and LPs in the last four years of his life; he also wrote exceptional new songs for him, which included "That's What Life Is All About," "Seasons" and "There's Nothing That I Haven't Sung About." By sheer coincidence and serendipity we listened that day while the master recording of "At My Time of Life" was being processed for duplication. Although the show that featured the song never made it to Broadway, it did become an important Crosby ballad and my sentimental favorite.

This yuletide the most popular recording of all time, Bing's timeless classic, "White Christmas," will once again be heard around the world. The film that introduced the perennial Irving Berlin ballad, *Holiday Inn*, co-starring Bing and Fred Astaire, was released for the holidays of 1942. Since that time the Crosby name has been synonymous with Christmas.

In the dark days of World War II, Allied servicemen affectionately called him "Santa Claus Without Whiskers" for he was the embodiment of the Christmas season. He lives on in our collective memory, for it is still not possible to think of Christmas without thinking of Bing.

The Crosby library of enduring Christmas songs reads like a Yuletide Hit Parade, "I'll Be Home for Christmas," "Santa Claus Is Coming to Town," "Christmas in Killarney," "Silver Bells," "Do You Hear What I Hear?" and "Jingle Bells," to name only a few. His recordings of traditional carols have lifted our hearts and spirits for six decades.

In 1973, in a December issue of *Variety*, the entertainment weekly, a feature story estimated that Bing's recording of "White Christmas" had sold well over 40 million copies. Typical of Bing's modest nature, he found that figure quite high, "That's hard to believe. I'll accept it and hope that Mr. Berlin gets adequately compensated. He's the one who wrote it and is responsible for its success."

With several re-issues over the past 20 years of his most famous recording, it is estimated now that its worldwide sales could be as high as 100 million. Whatever the figure, it is without question the best-selling record in the history of the music business.

During one of our conversations, a few weeks before Christmas 1974, Bing reflected on the impact of his most identifiable song: "I certainly didn't think 'White Christmas' was going to be such a hit. I thought it was a very good score for *Holiday Inn,* but I had no preconceived idea what would be the hit song. 'White Christmas' just stepped out, because it was wartime and so many people were away from home, away from their families, serving in the army, navy and air force and in faraway places—and a song like that is reminiscent of home and family, and that's why it had such an immediate and lasting impact, I believe."

Bing's musical conductor for many years, John Scott Trotter, was also the arranger on many of his most memorable recordings. I wondered if he ever had a feeling that one of their collaborations might be a hit. "When we made 'White Christmas' I thought it was a very lovely tune, but I had no idea that it would turn out to be the most famous recording of all time. However, working with Bing and knowing the depth of his public acceptance, there was always a good chance that any of our sessions would be successful."

He also recalled how the song might have been recorded in a different manner than its now familiar arrangement. "There was an argument between Jack Kapp, who was the head of Decca Records, and Irving Berlin. The song was written for a scene in the picture that was set on the west coast. The lyrics of the verse began, 'I'm sitting here in Beverly Hills'—Berlin thought it was a marvelous poetic set-up for the chorus, but Kapp said it had nothing to do with the record. Kapp prevailed and we didn't record the verse, and as luck would have it, the movie setting for the song was changed later from sunny California to snowy New England."

When Bing heard Trotter's comments he had no recollection of the difference of opinion between Kapp and Berlin. "I don't recall a controversy, Gord; I know we didn't do the verse, not even in the picture. In fact it was done quite simply, sitting at a piano in a ruminative mood. There was no production, just a chorus or two with the leading lady, Marjorie Reynolds."

Holiday Inn has been acclaimed by several critics and film historians as the best original movie musical ever made. The charming and amusing plot concerned a talented but weary entertainer (Crosby) who left his ambitious partner (Astaire) for the tranquility of a country inn, where he produced shows only on holidays! It was a magical teaming of the screen's two incomparable performers, who were in top form as they featured a Berlin melody for every holiday of the year. In 1954 another Crosby musical, filmed in technicolor with Rosemary Clooney and Danny Kaye, took as its title *White Christmas* and revived the time-honored song on its soundtrack.

While on his lengthy overseas tour in 1944, Bing couldn't do a show without bringing a little bit of home to the front lines with "White Christmas." At the time of our last interview his thoughts went back to those bitter-sweet wartime days. "Well, it was always a kind of a wrench for me to sing the song," he confessed. "I loved it of course, but at the camps and in the field hospitals, places where spirits weren't too high anyway, they'd ask for the song—they'd demand it—and half the audience would be in tears. It was a rather lugubrious atmosphere that it created, which you can understand, because of its connotation of home and Christmas, and here we were thousands of miles from either one. It was a rather sorrowing experience to have to sing it for these men and women when it made them feel sad. But I guess in retrospect that it was a glad kind of sadness."

Bing Crosby

In thinking back over his life and unparalleled career he made this final comment of appreciation and gratitude to his friends and fans: "To know that you have entertained, amused and made life a little more pleasant for people, wherever they happen to be, that's the greatest reward of all."

✪ ✪ ✪

At the podium, Gonzaga University, Spokane, Washington, as emcee of the unveiling of the bronze Bing Crosby statue. May 3, 1981. (Photo by D.H. Evahold, Spokane WA)

Below: The Crosby Bronze statue, Gonzaga University.

[*Editor's note: In 1976 Gord Atkinson's radio series* The Crosby Years *won a prestigious Armstrong Award from Columbia University of New York, and was honored by the American National Radio Broadcasters Association at their annual convention in San Francisco. Bing Crosby received a Lifetime Achievement Award that same evening.*

In 1981 Gord was the emcee at Gonzaga University, Spokane, Washington, for the unveiling of a bronze statue of Bing Crosby on the campus of his alma mater. The televised ceremony, which took place by the Crosby Library, was attended by Kathryn Crosby, family members, political figures and Bing Crosby's many friends, including Phil Harris, songwriter James Van Heusen, Rich Little—and over a thousand Crosby fans from around the world.]

EPILOGUE

In writing this book I have had the opportunity to pay tribute to a group of exceptional members of the show business community. I sincerely hope that you have enjoyed these personal accounts of their lives and careers. They have all made considerable contributions to the world of entertainment.

My only regret is that many of my favorite stars were not included in this book because of space limitations. However, I am pleased to inform you that a sequel is being planned by my publisher, Creative Bound.

Here are just a few of the stars who will be profiled in our next book: Julie Andrews, Lorne Greene, Dorothy Lamour, Liberace, Nana Mouskouri, Jack Benny, Judy Garland, Roger Whittaker, Wayne and Shuster, Peggy Lee, Andy Williams and Edgar Bergen and Charlie McCarthy. We will also re-visit some of the performers whose stories appear in this book for further insights into their fascinating careers.

Until then, I wish you "the very best of entertainment!"

Gord Atkinson

INDEX

Index

Index